Achieve your goals through persuasion

Eighty-five percent of your success depends upon your ability to communicate your ideas; in particular, your ability to persuade others to cooperate with you in producing the results you desire.

Dr. Robert Anthony's Magic Power of Super Persuasion will make you a superior communicator in all kinds of situations. You will understand people better and be able to communicate your ideas more effectively. As a result, you will be more competent in saying what you *mean* and meaning what you *say*. This is an essential quality of the Super Persuader.

It is also the essential key to success for top achievers everywhere . . .

DR. ROBERT ANTHONY'S
MAGIC POWER
OF SUPER PERSUASION

Most Berkley Books are available at special quantity discounts for bulk
purchases for sales promotions, premiums, fund raising, or educational
use. Special books or book excerpts can also be created to fit specific needs.

For details, write or telephone Special Markets, The Berkley Publishing
Group, 200 Madison Avenue, New York, New York 10016; (212) 951-8891.

DR. ROBERT ANTHONY'S
MAGIC
POWER
OF
SUPER
PERSUASION

BERKLEY BOOKS, NEW YORK

Based on a work made for oral delivery
entitled COMMUNICATE WITH SELF CONFIDENCE
copyright © 1973 by Dr. Robert Anthony

DR. ROBERT ANTHONY'S MAGIC
POWER OF SUPER PERSUASION

A Berkley Book / published by arrangement with
the author

PRINTING HISTORY
Berkley edition / July 1988

ISBN: 0-425-10981-X

A BERKLEY BOOK ® TM 757,375
Berkley Books are published by The Berkley Publishing Group,
200 Madison Avenue, New York, NY 10016.
The name "BERKLEY" and the "B" logo
are trademarks belonging to Berkley Publishing Corporation.

PRINTED IN THE UNITED STATES OF AMERICA

10   9   8   7   6   5

Table of Contents

Introduction

Eighty-five percent of your success depends upon your ability to communicate your ideas, in particular your ability to persuade others to cooperate with you in producing the results you desire.

The Magic Power of Super Persuasion will make you a superior communicator in all kinds of situations. You will understand people better and be able to communicate your ideas more effectively. As a result, you will be more competent in saying what you *mean*, and meaning what you *say.* This is an essential quality of the Super Persuader.

The Magic Power of Super Persuasion will help you to redesign your communication patterns and give you the edge over those who do not understand the principles of Super Persuasion. The principles in each chapter are easy to understand and easy to apply. Don't let the simplicity of the ideas fool you. You will be amazed how others are persuaded to your way of thinking as you apply the principles in your everyday communications.

The starting point of building your powers of Super Persuasion is to develop the self-confidence of the Super Persuader. To learn how, just turn the page!

Chapter 1
HOW TO BE
A SELF-CONFIDENT
SUPER PERSUADER

One of the most powerful tools for success is the ability to persuade others to believe you, to follow you, and to help you. Your ability to *persuade* is the basis of your ability to *get what you want*. We are finding that as modern life becomes more complicated, with more decisions to be made on a daily basis, those who can persuade others have a powerful advantage for achieving success.

The ability to win others to your point of view is invaluable. We can be far more successful in everyday situations—asking for a raise, settling a difference with a neighbor, helping your children make wise choices—if we use the communications techniques of great persuaders. But until recently even the best of them couldn't tell you what makes them persuasive. Now, after hundreds of studies, researchers have found that persuasiveness is greatly enhanced by *specific, identifiable* techniques that we can all use. Keep in mind that persuasion is *not* manipulation. It is, instead, creating the *right environment* for your ideas and then *communicating* those ideas effectively.

The ability to present yourself and your ideas well will determine your success in any given situation. In fact, without this ability, your skills and personality may go *unnoticed*. The Mellon Foundation did a study on those who are successful in life. They came to the conclusion that technical skills accounted for only 15% of the equation. Interpersonal skills—

the ability to communicate with others and get their cooperation—accounted for 85% of success. Imagine that, 85% of your success depends on your ability to communicate.

SUPER PERSUADERS HAVE THESE QUALITIES

Franklin D. Roosevelt said, "Not everything that is faced can be changed, but *nothing* can be changed until it is faced." Redesigning your communication patterns begins with sharpening your perceptions of others and yourself. Think for a moment of the public figures and personal acquaintances who have held your attention as they spoke. What qualities do you notice about them? How many of the following statements came to your mind? "They have confidence and ease, which in turn makes *me* feel at ease with *them*. They carry *authority* and *conviction* in their voice. They established *trust* and *credibility*, verbally and nonverbally. They are warm, animated, and *enthusiastic*. They show empathy and concern. They *look* at me and *pay attention* to me when I'm talking." All of these qualities add up to charisma. Those who have it command our attention. They know how to project the *best* of *themselves*. They exert a profound influence on others. A room lights up because they're in it.

All of these qualities are discussed in the following chapters, along with specific techniques that you can use immediately. Your communication skills will improve as you apply these suggestions to your everyday life. People in your life will *recognize* that you have become more understanding and charismatic. And the best part is that they'll be willing to give you a level of commitment *that will enable you to get what you want*.

SUPER PERSUASION STARTS WITH SELF-CONFIDENCE

Let's begin with the quality of *confidence*. The word has several definitions. A very apt definition is "to converse intimately with." In other words, if you have confidence in someone, you converse intimately with them. Taking this thought a step further, let's apply our definition to self-confidence, in the sense of intimately talking to *yourself*. It is that internal, private monologue that goes on in your mind. Follow me now, because this is important.

You are, in a very real sense, self-confident in everything you do, every minute you are awake. Maybe you have heard a statement about someone and you said, "They have a lot of self-confidence." But the truth is that *everyone* has a lot of self-confidence. There isn't even a single word in the dictionary that defines "*lack* of self-confidence."

The key point to be aware of is whether you are self-confident of your ability to *succeed* or you are self-confident about your ability to *fail*. Whichever route you are pursuing, you are talking intimately to yourself about it. And this self-talk *creates* your self-confidence—positive or negative. If you are talking intimately to yourself about depression, then you are absolutely self-confident about being depressed. If you are talking intimately to yourself about illness, you are absolutely self-confident about being ill. Whatever we are self-confident about is what we will experience. We might say that self-confidence creates results.

SUPER PERSUADER'S MENTAL PICTURE

Henry Ford said, "If you think you can or think you can't, you're right." Be careful what you *imagine* yourself becoming. There is an abundance of scientific evidence to support the assertion that your mental picture of yourself, more than anything else, determines your achievements. The brain is like an automatic guidance system. It will steer your life *toward* the mental self-image you enter into it. Your subconscious mind will work *for* you or *against* you. *You decide,* by putting in self-fulfilling *goals* or self-defeating *limitations*. In computer terms, they call it GIGO—garbage in, garbage out. Or perhaps a better way of saying it is: Good *thoughts* in, good *results* out. When this law is understood and applied, dynamic changes can take place. The good news is that unwanted, unworkable habits and behavior patterns *can* be altered. This can be achieved by creating positive self-confidence through a positive self-image.

FOUR QUALITIES OF A SELF-CONFIDENT PERSUADER

There are *four* outstanding qualities of a self-confident persuader. The first is *imagination*. You must imagine yourself as the person you want to become, taking your mind off the way you are now.

The second quality is *commitments* and can be summarized by the statement: "I will *until . . .*" How long does a baby commit himself to learn how to walk? *Until* he does! How long shall we commit ourselves to our goals? *Until* we reach them. There is a tremendous amount of energy that is available for you to use. Simply give up asking yourself, "Will I or won't I?" "Can I or can't I?" Know that YOU CAN and that YOU WILL— *until*. This is an unconditional, nonnegotiable commitment. Nothing can stop the power of a *totally committed* person.

So, *first* you imagine. Then you *commit*. The third step is affirmation; *affirm* that you will succeed. It helps to verbalize your positive thinking—self-talk. This will raise your self-confidence and thus cause *others* to believe in your eventual success. Now an amazing thing happens. As *other* people start *believing* in you, they'll want to *help* you. This adds even more to your self-confidence in succeeding. How often have you heard, "Nothing succeeds like success"? Now you know why that is so.

The fourth quality is *persistence*. *Never give up*. This is one of my favorites! *Patience* and *persistence* are *key* to achieving anything. Make a decision that defeat and failure are not even worth your attention.

EXPECTATIONS INCREASE OR DECREASE YOUR PERFORMANCE

Negative thoughts are picked up from a variety of sources. Perhaps you have an *inferiority complex* because you did poorly in school. Maybe you have decided that you're not very bright. Don't believe it! You may have had a poor teacher.

Harvard psychologist Robert Rosenthal wondered if some children performed poorly in school because their teachers *expected* them to. If that's so, Rosenthal surmised, then raising the teacher's *expectations* should raise the children's *performance*. He put together a plan to try his theory in real classrooms. Students in kindergarten through fifth-grade at a cooperating school were given a new test of learning ability. The following September, after the tests were graded, the teachers were given the names of five or six children who were identified as "spurters," those who possessed exceptional learning ability.

What the teachers didn't know was that the names had been chosen on a *random basis* even before the tests were given. The difference between those chosen and the rest of the students existed only in the minds of the teachers.

The same test was given at the end of the school year. It showed that the spurters had actually soared far ahead of the other children. They gained as many as fifteen to twenty-seven IQ points. The teachers described these children as being happier, more curious, and affectionate, and as having a better chance to be successful in later life. Obviously the *only* change had been one of *attitudes*. Because the teachers *expected* more of these children, they came to expect more of *themselves*.

Rosenthal said that the explanation probably lies in the *subtle interactions* between the teacher and pupils. Even though a teacher may be unaware of the unconscious signals they are sending, tone of voice, facial expression, touch, and posture all communicate expectations. Such communication may very well help a child by changing his perceptions of himself.

Remember, Goethe said, "Treat people as if they were what they *ought to be* and you help them to become what they are capable of *being*." [author's italics] This is also true of what you say and think about *yourself*.

SUPER PERSUADERS LEARN TO CONQUER FEAR

Whenever the attention is centered on us, we are apt to become uneasy or self-conscious. Being the *focus* of attention tends to be unnerving. When you're conscious of the self, you tend to focus your self-confidence on your negative aspects. The mere fact that someone is looking on, perhaps critically, often causes you to lose your poise and become aware of your limitations. Fear creeps in. Fear is the process you *set up* to protect yourself. An example of this is a talented artist who avoids pursuing his talent for fear that he'll be a failure in the eyes of others. Fear causes you to *say* and *do* things that you'd rather not *express*. It makes you feel *awkward* and *uncomfortable* when you'd rather be *relaxed* and *poised*. Everyone wants to get rid of fear. Wouldn't you rather walk into any situation with your head held high, with a feeling of assurance?

Now, we aren't talking about cockiness. Confidence is the feeling of *assurance* about life. It is an inward *knowledge* that you can handle any circumstance. Cockiness or conceit is trying to convince *others* when you really have doubts about your own abilities. It's being insecure and whistling in the dark. Cockiness reveals a greater insecurity than just feeling self-conscious.

One of the fears that causes you to doubt yourself is the fear of failure. Each person wants to *succeed*. Think about an athlete. Maybe he wants to succeed so much that he develops a fear that something will happen to cause him to fail. This fear of failure can affect him in two ways. It may spur him on to greater achievement. But if he gives in to the fear and becomes self-confident that he will fail, his *ability* will surely begin to slip away.

We have another fear. It is the fear of appearing ridiculous or foolish. Giving in to this fear, causes many people to doubt themselves. We all want to appear poised. We want to appear self-assured. But so many little things happen in our lives that make us look ridiculous. Holding fast to a confidence in your abilities—and developing a good *sense of humor*—can help you get through the most embarrassing moments.

Another fear is the fear of exposing the ego to hurt. The ego is the little outer self, the personality, that we have developed over the years. The word *personality* comes from the Latin word *persona*. It means "mask." Personality is the mask or facade that we present to the world, hoping that the world will think it's real. We don't want anyone looking behind the mask, only to find what we fear is a quivering, insecure person. So we often live in fear that the ego will be hurt or exposed. And we will go to almost any extent to protect it.

Another fear is the fear of being *rejected*. Think of a shy young man about to ask a girl for a date. We see him—red in the face, stammering, and thoroughly embarrassed. We might laugh it off, but it's no joke to him. He has the fear of being rejected and pushed away. The fear of being rejected is very *prevalent*. Because of it, some people are afraid to make friends and take risks, and so, in seeking to protect themselves from possible rejection, they lead very lonely lives.

Psychologists have found that this fear of rejection is one of the common, key trouble spots in marital relationships. Because of this fear, one partner may not give the whole self to the marriage. There is a holding back. A good marriage must be based on 100% giving from each partner. It can't be the attitude of "I want your love and devotion, as much as I can get; but I won't give you mine for fear I will get hurt." We hear a lot about fifty-fifty giving in marriage. But it's not *enough*. Fifty-fifty giving is still a *contest*, based on self-protection.

A part of the fear of rejection is the fear that loss of approval is in every phase of human existence. This fear explains why people tend to shrink away from expressing original thoughts and conform blindly to the average thinking of the *majority*. In our society we have a fetish to be "normal." A person trying to be "normal" will lose confidence in his ability to think for himself and lose his true identity. How much more rewarding it is to be *natural* rather than *normal!*

SELF-CONSCIOUS OR SELF-CONFIDENT?

We've covered the things that may be holding you back, the reasons why you may feel self-conscious. What is the key to developing the self-confidence necessary to achieve your goal in communication? It is *authenticity,* the discovery of the awesome power derived simply from your ability to *be yourself*. Many critics think that being *yourself* will lead to *selfishness*. But authenticity doesn't do this. It *starts* from the center of your life, but it is not *self-centered*. It sets a glowing example for others and sets them into action. This is a dynamic natural power that's available to *all* of us.

AUTHENTICITY—THE KEY TO PERSUASION

Authenticity makes your life count because it restores power to the individual. To be yourself is a natural, human, and universal power. And it brings tremendous blessings.

A client recently said to me in pure frustration, "If only I could 'find myself'!" I smiled and said, "George, if you 'found yourself,' who would you be?"

He thought for a moment and then said, "I'd be like John Smith. He has a good position in his company. He's well-respected in the community. He's a good golfer and he has lots of friends. His wife and kids love him, and he gets a new car every year."

"Hold it!" I responded. "You wouldn't be finding *yourself*. You would be finding John Smith. And since you'd be the same, you would cancel each other out!" There's a definite difference between *finding* yourself and *knowing* yourself. Observe other people and what you like about them. And then adapt those qualities as a part of your behavior. Shakespeare wrote, "Assume a virtue and it's yours." However, do not try to mold yourself to be exactly like someone else. Celebrate your own uniqueness and talents.

Today there are many books written about assertiveness and manipulation. But in our society the assertive manipulators do not win as often as you might think. Many companies are headed by *authentic* people. They've risen to the top because others are *drawn* to them, *admire* them, and *imitate* their example. Think about a businessman you know, one who has risen to the top over others who seem to be more clever.

Why has *he* succeeded? His associates may say that he's "fairer to deal with" or that he has "a greater vision." But it is more than that. He has an inner strength. He radiates confidence in *who he is* and where he is going. He is *instinctively honest*. And he never weakens his moral authority with *dishonest compromise*.

Take note: Authentic people know what they want and where they want to go. Often, in pursuit of their goals, they will stand up to ridicule in order to accomplish something *they* believe in. Albert Schweitzer, the great missionary doctor, had that experience at a very early age. When he was a boy, his friends proposed that they go up in the hills and kill birds. Albert was reluctant; afraid of being laughed at, he went along. They arrived at a tree in which a whole flock of birds was singing. The boys put stones in their slingshots. Albert could not stand the thought of killing any living thing. He shooed the birds away and left for home. From that day on, reverence for life was more important to him than the fear of being laughed at. His priorities were clear.

Fatigue is a common symptom of people who have suppressed who they really are. They are not really tired, but tired *of*. It takes a lot of effort *not* to be ourselves. We become actors playing a role, trying to impress other people, and that's very hard work! By contrast, the authentic person does not give energy to contradictions. His actions are consistent with his inner self. His self-honesty reduces internal conflicts. He feels alive and exhilarated. His energy is turned on by doing what matters to him. He doesn't dissipate energy on conflicts or deceits.

The authentic person also *mobilizes* the energy of *others*. He inspires them. Just by being himself, he makes a statement about what one needs to do to succeed. Someone who respects and likes himself can respect and like others. When we are not sure who we are, we are uneasy. We try to find out what the other person would *like* us to say before we speak. We try to find out what they want us to do before we act. When we are insecure, our relationships to others are governed by what *we* need rather than what *they* need. On the other hand, authentic people are out not only for themselves, but for others too. No energy is wasted in protecting a shaky ego.

Growing in authenticity means *becoming* more of what we're truly meant to be. It's a process we learn day by day. Perhaps you deny yourself the pleasure of your own good moments. If you let it, the power of *your own* acknowledgment and appreciation can drive home the experience—and satisfaction—of success. This is the foundation for expanding to more positive experiences.

Here is a very simple thing you can do. Take time at the end of your day to appreciate the good moments in it. If you did something well, *allow* yourself to feel *pleased* about it. It might have been a small thing that would not have meant much to anyone else, but it was not easy for you. Perhaps you were nervous about meeting someone for the first time. Perhaps you made a difficult phone call. Perhaps you settled a misunderstanding. Whatever it was, close your eyes and concentrate on the pleasure of that small achievement. You are nourishing yourself in the most practical way. You are feeding your positive expectations. And next time it will be *easier*. After a while the good moments will become the major part of your day.

FIVE ACTION STEPS TO INCREASE YOUR ABILITY TO BE A SELF-CONFIDENT SUPER PERSUADER

1. Project self-confidence even when it is not there. The phrase to remember is *act as if*. Act as if you have *already* achieved your goal and it is yours. The world supports people who know where they're going.

2. Accept the idea that nothing is wrong in being different from other people. The truth is, all of

us are different, and we are meant to be different. Often, under the guise of "finding ourselves," we vainly attempt to *imitate* others. Emerson said that imitation is suicide. Instead of imitating, celebrate your uniqueness.

3. "Props" can be self-confidence boosters. In *The Devil's Advocate,* Morris West tells of one character who simply put a fresh carnation in the lapel of his coat and faced the world with confidence! A different hairstyle, a new set of clothes, or trimming off a few pounds can transform you from a self-degrading to a self-complimenting person.

4. People who inspire you can do wonders in bolstering your self-confidence. Seek out the friendship and surround yourself with people who have a high, positive self-regard, rather than associating with those who always put themselves down.

5. Spend some time with yourself. Solitude is at the heart of self-knowledge. It is when we are alone that we learn to distinguish between the false and the true. Shakespeare wrote, "to thine own self be true . . . thou canst not then be false to any man." To *know yourself* is the basis of powerful communication. And everything that is free from *falsehood* is strength. To know yourself is to know *everyone!*

And so you are to be congratulated. You have taken that important first step in becoming more authentic in your communications. You will understand people better and communicate your ideas more clearly and firmly as you progress through this book. A journey of a thousand miles begins with a single step. And you are now on your way to learning how to communicate with greater self-confidence!

Chapter 2

SUPER PERSUASION—
THE FIRST FOUR
MINUTES

Emerson wrote, "What you are speaks so loudly I can't hear what you are saying." This is especially true when we consider first impressions. The first two to four minutes that you spend with a person are more important than any other four minutes that you will ever have together.

You make first impressions every day. You *succeed* or *fail* by the impressions you make in interviews, telephone calls, meetings, presentations, and thousands of business and social encounters. Power, trust, and credibility are given to those who make good impressions. If people aren't quickly attracted to you, or if they don't like what they see and hear in those first few moments, they probably will not pay attention to all the *words* that you are using to show your knowledge and authority.

During your first few moments of interaction with others, their attention span and powers of retention are the highest. They are completely focused on *you*. The process of creating impressions is somewhat predictable. Depending on the background and expectations of the other person and the context of your meeting, these are the things that psychologists tell us that people notice first.

FOUR TRAITS THAT OTHERS NOTICE FIRST

First of all, in any first encounter, people zero in on what they *see*. In fact, there is a specific order that people use to process information about you. Those you meet will notice the color of your skin, your gender and age, your appearance and facial expressions, the eye contact you maintain, body movements, personal space, and touch. Vast amounts of information are conveyed in this nonverbal exchange. In fact, communication experts agree that the nonverbal accounts for more than *half* of your *total* message. A surprising 55% of the meaning of your message is conveyed by facial expressions and body language alone.

Next, people notice what they *hear*. They listen to characteristics of your voice—the rate or tempo, loudness, pitch, articulation, and tone, all of which reveal more information about you. In fact, your voice—and this does not include the *words* you are saying—may transmit as much as 38% of the *meaning* of your message. On the telephone it conveys even more, because the other person cannot see what you look like.

You should be aware that the *last* thing people notice about you, and therefore the *least* important for a first impression, are the *words* you are using. The words contribute only 7% to the meaning of your message. It's not that your words are unimportant. They *are* important. But in order for them to be heard, the other person must first like what he sees and what he hears. His mind may already be made up before you speak. And that first impression is indelibly formed.

Throughout this entire process the other person is gathering bits and pieces of information to form a composite picture of you. He reads and processes all of these things, fits them into his own belief system, and comes out with an impression of who he thinks you are. The purpose of this chapter is to give you information and techniques to help you send the true message. So much of what we do is unconscious, and you may be sending erroneous or conflicting information to the people you meet.

WHAT DO YOU LOOK LIKE TO OTHERS?

Let's consider what you look like. Most people cannot recognize themselves when their own image is unexpectedly reflected back to them. They have trouble remembering what they look like. Likewise, they are not aware of their body language. Remember, words contribute only 7% to the meaning of your message; whether or not you are actually speaking, you're always *communicating!*

The range of situations in which first impressions are *helped* or *hindered* by appearance and body language is great. For example, teachers with a positive outlook will use nonverbal cues to encourage student involvement. They smile and nod, listen actively, and encourage physical closeness. Teachers with a negative attitude use their nonverbal cues to discourage involvement. They smile less, occupy greater personal space to keep the kids farther away, and avoid direct eye contact.

Nonverbal communication, including everything from appearance to facial expression to movement, are what other people use to judge *attractiveness*. Studies show that physically attractive people are perceived to be more intelligent, more likable, more interesting, and more credible than those who present a less attractive impression.

Also, people who are sensitive to *nonverbal cues* tend to be better adjusted, more extroverted and popular, more effective in personal relationships, better listeners, and less dogmatic. Therefore, becoming more aware of your *own* body language has the additional benefit of allowing you to see *others* in a new light.

One useful technique for becoming more aware of how you present yourself is to watch a film clip or video of yourself to see what you really look like. Or look into a mirror and then see if you can write a description that would pick you out in a roomful of people. Now keep in mind that the first impression you make will be filtered through the perceptions of another person according to his expectations, the context of your meeting, and your communication display.

Some aspects of nonverbal communication are easily *changed,* such as appearance and, less easily, facial expression. Others are easily *controlled,* such as gestures. And others are *beyond control,* such as gender and skin color.

Despite attempts to overcome prejudices, skin color still remains the dominant factor of appearance. In situations where you think your skin color may be a negative factor, seek to counter stereotypes by paying extra attention to your appearance, facial expressions, and eye contact.

Gender also fosters stereotypes. Being *male* carries more power and authority in first encounters. Men are usually given more credibility. To compensate, a woman can signal her savvy and authority by being prompt, having a strong handshake, maintaining direct eye contact, and using a smile to counter any excessive aggressiveness.

Age, in and of itself, is neither positive nor negative; its relevance depends entirely on the *expectations* of the other person. If you think you might look *too old,* do these things: wear clothing that is stylish but not too trendy; have a modern hairstyle; move and gesture with energy and vitality. For those who feel they look *too young,* here are some suggestions: dress more conservatively; avoid long hair; carry quality accessories; and use makeup that does not draw attention to your face.

Appearance includes much more than dress or clothing. It also takes into account your body type, posture, hair, accessories that you both wear and carry, smells, and the color of your clothing and makeup. In creating the right image, you need to consider three things: What are the others' *expectations?* What will create the image *I want?* Am I *comfortable* with the *results?* Remember, anytime you violate expectations, you assume risks. One of the risks is a negative first impression.

After your overall general appearance, your face is the most visible part of you. Facial expressions are the cue most people use to pick up on your mood and personality. It is critical for your facial expressions to be congruent with the tone of voice and the words being spoken. When the message from all three communication channels is *mixed*, then your face will be *ignored* and your tone of voice believed.

A rule of thumb for effective eye contact is to make it direct but to adjust it according to the *comfort* level. In situations where you are dealing with white men (regardless of whether you are a woman, a minority male, or another white male), direct eye contact throughout the interaction is usually best.

Movement is a critical aspect in the presentation of a confident, assured impression. This is because your walk and posture are tied closely to your *emotional* state. Those people in conflict will have jerky, disjointed movements. Signs of depression and alienation are slumped posture and shuffling movements. Stress and anxiousness are shown in frenetic, rushed walks or gestures. People who are sure of themselves have energetic, purposeful movements. They look strong and confident.

People who are confident take up more personal space and freely move into the space of others. *Less* confident people actually *yield* space to others. To give an impression of power, *occupy more space* when you stand or sit, and do not move out of the way or allow invasion of your space by those attempting to dominate you.

Keep in mind, however, that ours is a noncontact culture. The consequences of touching are often risky and subject to a lot of different interpretations. A firm handshake is, then, the safest, least controversial, and most equitable form of touch when meeting someone for the first time.

WHAT DO YOU SOUND LIKE TO OTHERS?

Speech plays a vital role in making first impressions. The people we meet don't know if their initial impressions are valid, so they will listen intently for other clues. What you sound like to others can have a lasting impact. Deep, diaphragmatic breathing is essential to achieve a strong, pleasant voice. With that as a basis, there are five qualities that you can adjust to create a favorable impression with your voice.

1. *Vary the rate.* When you're meeting someone who has never heard you, start slowly if you are a fast talker, and build to your normal rate. Use the pause effectively. Silence can help you stress your point and build interest.

2. *Control the loudness.* The level of loudness you employ should be determined by your distance from the listeners, environmental noises, the situation, and the material.

3. *Fine-tune the pitch.* Here there are several things to avoid: a rising or upward inflection at the ends of sentences; a singsong quality; monotony; and a booming voice (rain-barrel effect) signals gruffness or hostility.

4. *Monitor vocal quality.* Voice quality gives clear proof how relaxed or tense you are. It reveals self-confidence or self-consciousness. Negative features that detract from tonal quality are nasality, breathiness, thinness, stridency, harshness, and hoarseness. To overcome these negative qualities, open your mouth more, breathe from your diaphragm and relax your throat and neck muscles.

5. Finally, *articulate your words clearly.*

These five aspects can be improved or modified by listening to a tape recording of yourself. If possible, it's best to record your voice when you're interacting with other people, perhaps at a party or a gathering. A thirty-minute tape will give you enough feedback to know exactly what areas need improvement. After that, it's just a matter of practicing the techniques until you are satisfied with the results.

HOW SUPER PERSUADERS USE PACING

People who are very skilled at making good impressions and developing rapport use a technique called *pacing*. This means meeting the other person *where he is* and reflecting back to him what he knows to be true. You can pace a person's mood and body language. Also, you can pace his speech patterns: his rate of speech, volume, intonations, words, phrases, and vocabulary. You can even pace his energy level. And, of course, you can pace his beliefs and opinions.

We tend to like people who are like us. Research strongly suggests that we affiliate with people like ourselves. We tend to *hire* people like ourselves. When you pace and mirror back body language, you communicate, "I'm okay—you can trust me." When you pace voice or speech patterns, you are saying, "I'm on your wavelength." If you don't pace the other person, at least initially, the message is, "I'm *different* from you. I'm *not* on your wavelength. Maybe you can't trust me." Pacing is something that we do all the time. It is not making fun of the other person; rather, it is being attentive enough to vary your responses to match his, which will in turn make him more comfortable.

Life moves so fast today that you're certain to meet someone new every day. For more than just pleasant conversations, let's talk about how you can initiate productive communication. This means that when you are with a stranger, you have to decide how to talk to him or her.

WINNING OVER A STRANGER

The easiest way is to appeal to his *interests*. Salespeople must do this every day. Before they give you a big sales pitch on a new car, they need to find out if you are interested in a station wagon, a sedan, or, if you're in a mid-life crisis, a sports car. Even though you may not be selling anything, you are still faced with the same problem—finding out what topics interest the other person and which ones don't. The best way to do this is to act like a salesman and ask questions. Don't waste your time guessing. It's so much *easier* to let the other person *tell* you. Then all you have to do is lead a discussion about these interests. For example, let's say you would like to get to know a new neighbor. You might begin by an observation: "I notice that your car is usually gone by the time I leave for the office. Do you have to drive very far to work?" This can lead to a conversation about what the person does and many other interesting facts.

Another beginning is to appeal to his *emotions*. All of us have strong emotions as a basic part of our personality. Carefully observe the other person as he's talking. Keep your eyes and ears open and you'll be surprised at the insights that you get into his feeling. You can pick up very quickly on his likes and dislikes. When the emotions are *positive,* his eyes will be brighter and more excited, and his voice will sound more enthusiastic. *Negative* emotions are shown by a discouraged tone of voice and a slight pulling away or tensing of his muscles when he talks about certain things.

You can do this when you focus your full attention on the reactions, feelings, and words of the other person and *not* on your own *thoughts*. Don't worry about what *you* will say. Think only about what *he's* communicating to *you*, both *verbally* and *nonverbally*. If you do this, you will always know automatically what to say next.

HOW TO "READ" OTHERS IN THE FIRST FEW MINUTES

When you're with strangers, there are some shortcuts that you can use to get clues about the other person. Practice using these skills and you'll be amazed at how adept you will become at sizing people up.

Suppose you've just met someone, made a few friendly comments, and then stopped to give him a turn to speak. And there was only silence! It's awkward, because he is very quiet and has given the lead right back to *you* again. Don't let the silence bother you. Instead, you can ask yourself some questions to find out why he is quiet.

1. Ask yourself, "Is he quiet because that's the way he *wants* to be?" Many quiet people are very smart and have the ability to hold good conversations, but they are reserved and don't speak until they have a good reason. You can continue by searching out his interests—"I notice that you're wearing a Dallas Cowboys T-shirt. Are you a rabid fan like me?" If he starts talking, you've broken through his shyness. If your first three or four questions get very short answers that say, "I'm not interested," then back away. Chances are he wants to be *alone* right now and doesn't want to talk to *anyone*.

2. Ask yourself, "Is he a perfectionist?" This kind of quiet person has very strong opinions about almost everything. He's usually set in his ways and doesn't tolerate people who do not think and talk the way he does. He always lets someone else take the lead in the conversation, and then lets them make the mistakes. Most people avoid talking to this kind of person. But sometimes you're in a situation where you must. Just go very slowly, looking for safe topics to talk about, and avoiding those that aren't "safe."

3. Ask yourself, "Is he waiting to be encouraged?" There are many quiet, down-to-earth people who want to join in but hesitate. Take the lead, in this case, with a lot of enthusiasm, and they are sure to join in on the fun.

4. Ask yourself, "Is he hiding a feeling of inferiority?" Some people have built up their weaknesses to be so big in their minds that their thinking causes them to believe that they aren't as good as everyone else. Some people express this as being very quiet. Others may cover up the inferiority by talking in a dominating way. If you get a feeling that he's really feeling inferior and trying to cover it up, be a good listener and let *him* take the lead. He'll sense your understanding and appreciate you for it.

INTELLECTUAL LEVEL DETERMINES RESPONSE

We also judge strangers very quickly on their intellectual level. This will determine how you respond to another individual. Here's what to look for: People with far above average intelligence tend to read a great deal—be it literature, science, or philosophy—and they usually talk with other intellectuals. They have a hard time bringing their vocabulary down to talk to an average person. The best way to communicate is to be *yourself*. If you're an intellectual, talk on the same vocabulary level as his. If you are an average person, listen carefully, for there's a lot you can learn. If you're having trouble understanding, admit it and ask questions so he can reexplain his idea in a way you can understand. You will win his respect by relaxing and being yourself, because he will see right through you if you talk about things that you know nothing about.

Not everyone who sounds like an intellectual is one. Sometimes you'll meet a person who is putting on an act, either because he's insecure or because he wants to impress you. You can tell if he uses big words and fancy expressions when they aren't really needed. Again, the best way to react is to be yourself. Realize that he's probably insecure, so put him at ease by keeping calm, relaxed, and natural. Use simple language. Show respect for him as a person. Soon he'll get the message that you're giving him between the lines: that there's no need for the put-on because you like him and accept him as he is. Chances are that he'll relax and talk naturally.

HANDLING THE STRONG-WILLED PERSON

What type of approach should you take with a strong-willed person? It depends on what you want to achieve in the conversation. Let's assume that you have a good idea and you want to convince other people.

If you are dealing with a basically aggressive person (and this doesn't always mean the same as "strong-willed"), you don't want to push too hard. Don't compete with him for control. Rather, tell him about the idea, then start pointing out a few things that may be wrong with it. The aggressive person usually reacts by *defending* the idea and tries to convince *you* that it's good. Usually, as long as he is in control, he doesn't care whose idea it is. If you are dealing with a quiet, sensitive person, on the other hand, act *unsure* about the idea and ask for his *advice*. He'll consider your idea a long time before giving his opinion, but if it's a good idea, he'll sell himself. If you are talking to someone who has a hard time reaching a decision, tell him *why* the idea is good, and how he can *benefit* from it. Then assume that he's ready to go along with it and assure him that he has made a good decision. If you are talking to a strong-willed, independent thinker, he will need to make his *own* decision. Describe your idea in the most *factual* and *dramatic* way that you can, to put the odds in your favor, and then let him make his decision. Strong-willed people must believe that they *alone* have made the decision.

Everyone is self-centered to some degree, so it's only a matter of time before you bump into someone's ego. If you are talking to a low-ego person, just give him the courtesy and attention you normally would. Show him sincere interest and honest respect. To deal with someone with a highly developed ego, if your intention is to win his goodwill, there are three things you can do: listen more than you talk; talk only about subjects that interest him; and compliment him at least two or three times.

Conversations would be a lot more fun if we didn't have to talk to chronically negative people. Unfortunately you may meet them on the job and in social situations. The easiest thing for you to do in this case is to steer the conversation away from personal problems.

Some people you meet will be open to others, and others will be closed-minded. One common trait of the closed-minded person is that he forms opinions on a whim and rarely looks for the facts. Once his opinion is formed, he'll hold on to it for dear life! Also, the closed-minded person will often think in a very petty way and be unconcerned with anything not directly related to him. Keep your conversation neutral and don't challenge his opinions.

The open-minded person sees what is going on around him and has a curiosity as to *why* it happens; he is objective. He will form strong opinions; but is more than willing to *change* his opinion if you can give sufficient information to show that *your* point of view is *right*. Present all the facts that you can that are relevant, and he'll carefully weigh them and change his opinion if he's wrong.

FIVE ACTION STEPS TO INSURE SUCCESS IN THE FIRST FOUR MINUTES

1. Decide what kind of impression you would like to make and what it will take to create that impression. Pay special attention to your personal appearance. Develop a professional-looking wardrobe and dress for the position you would like to have, not the one you have now.

2. Use direct eye contact and show sincere interest and honest acceptance to the people to whom you are talking.

3. Be consistent in all three communication channels—body, voice, and words. Incongruency implies insincerity.

4. Monitor your nonverbal cues. Gesture with purpose and always toward your viewer. Walk briskly. Stand and sit tall. You will feel more confident, and your voice will sound strong and resonant.

5. Be a good listener and pace your responses, body movements, and voice to the other person. Make sure that he realizes that the two of you are more alike than different.

Remember that you cannot *not* communicate. Everything you do or say, *don't* do or say, communicates something, whether it be positive or negative. With these suggestions you can communicate more effectively and understand better those who communicate with you. And as the fortune cookie says, "You only have one chance to make a good first impression."

Chapter 3
BODY SIGNALS OF THE SUPER PERSUADER

To begin our discussion on body signals or nonverbal communication, let's follow a typical middle-class American married male through his day to show how he produces and processes nonverbal human communication. First of all, he begins each day by preparing himself as a nonverbal message to the world: He shaves (unless, to present a different image, he has grown a full beard); he uses toothpaste, soap, and deodorant to send out messages of *smell;* he may then add aftershave or cologne; he combs his hair into a style that is current, or at least acceptable to those he meets. Some of his friends may wear hairpieces to look more youthful or more stylish. The costume may be topped off with a display of jewelry— wedding ring, class ring, tie tack, or gold chains. The jewelry can be used to display wealth, taste, political leaning, or to define the situation (work, leisure, formal, casual). Both his male and female friends use an array of cosmetics to enhance their best features, to cover blemishes, and to accent the features that are currently popular.

A person dresses not only for protection from the elements; his clothes are a *statement* about himself. And so we match our outfits to the events of the day: play or work, formal or informal, important or unimportant. Our dress reflects the way we feel about ourselves, the way we feel generally: happy or sad, youthful or mature, fashionable or conservative. Our clothing may accent our *best* features or *remold* those that are not so great.

While dressing, our typical American male may be listening to music or watching TV. Breakfast is announced by the smell of bacon and eggs or the aroma of coffee. Or perhaps his breakfast comes from very bright, colorful packages. His wife's facial expression may tell him whether he should talk, or read the paper. It may also determine whether he will compliment her or complain.

At work, he interacts with friends and associates by shaking their hands to communicate a *greeting* or an *agreement*. He nods to friends and waves to associates. He shows *approval* with a smile and *disapproval* with a frown. As he verbalizes, he talks with his hands. He regulates his interactions with a complex pattern of eye contact, head nods, and body movements. He also decodes the body movements of others: their status, their likes or dislikes, or their willingness to communicate. He meets people and makes immediate judgments about their competency and honesty. He makes persuasive attempts to present himself with his best foot forward.

He returns home *pleased* or *displeased* about what his home has to say about his station in life. He notices the *order* or *disorder* of the room and tries to detect the odor coming from the kitchen. He hugs his wife and then relaxes in front of the TV. He knows the theme song to his favorite show, and that the good guys wear white hats. The background music tells him when to feel tension or suspense. Perhaps his wife is wearing his favorite perfume and gives him a seductive look. This may bring about a whole set of courtship and touching behaviors, or it may bring about a *most eloquent nonverbal snore*.

IT'S IMPOSSIBLE NOT TO COMMUNICATE

The above example shows the impossibility of not communicating. Each of us is a transmitter that is impossible to shut off. No matter what we do, we send out messages about ourselves. The fact that you, and everyone around you, are constantly sending out nonverbal clues is important because it means that you have a constant source of information available about yourself and others. If you can tune in to these signals, you'll be more aware of *how* those around you are *feeling* and *thinking,* and you'll be better able to respond to what they *say.*

Knowing that people express their feelings by their actions is important to keep in mind when you notice that someone is often expressing, simultaneously, different or contradictory messages in their verbal and nonverbal behavior. A common example of this sort of "double message" is the experience we've all had of hearing someone with a red face and bulging veins yelling, "Angry? No, I'm not angry!" As we discuss the different kinds of nonverbal communication throughout this chapter, I'll also point out a number of ways in which people contradict themselves by conscious and unconscious behaviors. What you'll gain is a better idea of how others feel, even when they can't or won't tell you with their words.

HOW TO UNDERSTAND AND USE "PERSONAL SPACE"

We each walk around inside a kind of private bubble that represents the amount of airspace we feel we must have between ourselves and other people. This can be easily demonstrated by moving in gradually on another person. At some point the other person will begin, *irritably* or *absentmindedly*, to back away. Edward Hall, a professor from Northwestern University, first commented on these strong feelings about personal space and has developed the study of proxemics— the study of how man unconsciously structures microspace. Hall has hypothesized a whole scale of distances, each felt to be appropriate in this country for a particular kind of relationship.

Intimate distance is contact from actual touching, up to 18 inches apart. This is the distance for such interactions as wrestling or lovemaking or intimate talk. At this range people communicate not only by words but also by touch, smell, and body heat. Each person is aware of how fast the other is breathing, and of changes in the color and texture of the skin. A proximity between 1½ to 2½ feet is what Hall calls *personal* distance. It approximates the size of the personal-space bubble in a noncontact culture such as ours. A wife can comfortably stand inside her husband's bubble, but she may feel uneasy if another woman tries it. A distance of 2½ to 4 feet, within arm's length, for most people, is still considered within the range of personal distance, but it is the limit of physical domination. This far range of personal distance is appropriate for discussing personal matters.

A distance of 4 to 7 feet is called *close social* distance. In an office, people who work together normally stand this far apart to talk. *Far-phase* social distance, 7 to 12 feet, goes with formal conversation. Desks of important people are usually big enough to hold visitors at this distance. Above 12 feet, one gets into *public* distances, appropriate for speech making and for very formal styles of speaking.

Hall believes that human beings not only have strong feelings about *space* but also a real biological need for enough elbow room. Crowding definitely influences behavior, and it influences men and women differently. Men, when crowded together in a small room, tend to become suspicious and combative. Women tend to become friendlier and more intimate with one another; they're apt to like each other *better* and to find the whole experience *more pleasant* than if the meeting had been convened in a larger room.

Psychological studies have shown that people choose to stand closer to someone they like than to someone they don't. Friends stand closer together than acquaintances do, and acquaintances closer together than strangers. Space, then, communicates. When a number of people cluster together in a conversational group (at a party, for example) each individual expresses his position in the group near which he stands. When the group settles into a particular configuration and all the shifting has stopped, it's a sign that nonverbal negotiations are over. All concerned have arrived at a general (but not permanent) agreement on the level of intimacy that's to be maintained. The way people use space can communicate a good deal about power and status relationships. Generally we grant people with *higher* status *more* personal territory and greater privacy.

By observing the way people position themselves, you can learn a good deal about how they *feel*. Next time you're in a crowded room where people can choose whom to face directly, try observing who seems to be *included* in the action and who is being subtly *shut out*. And in the same way, pay attention to your own body orientation. You may be surprised to discover that you're avoiding a certain person without being conscious of it, or that at times you're turning your back on people altogether. If this is the case, it may be helpful to figure out *why*. Are you avoiding an unpleasant situation that needs clearing up, communicating annoyance or dislike for the other, or sending some other message? The general rule is, facing someone directly signals your interest, and facing *away* signals a desire to avoid involvement.

HOW POSTURE AND GESTURES INFLUENCE COMMUNICATION

Another way we communicate nonverbally is through our posture. The main reason we miss most posture messages is because they aren't very obvious. It's seldom that a person who feels weighted down by a problem hunches over so much that he stands out in a crowd. And when we're bored, we usually don't lean back and slump enough to embarrass the other person. The key is to look for small changes that might be indications of the way people feel inside.

I work hard to make my talks entertaining, but nobody's perfect, and I do have my off days. I can tell when I'm not doing a good job of communicating by picking out two or three people in different parts of the audience before I start my talk and watching how they sit throughout my presentation. As long as they're leaning forward, I know I'm doing okay, but if I see them starting to slump back, I know I'd better change my approach.

In addition to indicating interest or boredom, postures can also be a key to feelings of tension and relaxation. We take relaxed postures in nonthreatening situations and tighten up when threatened. Thus we can tell a good deal about how others feel simply by watching how tense or loose they seem to be.

Gestures are another good source of nonverbal communication. Most of us, at least unconsciously, know that the face is the most obvious channel of expressing emotions, and so we're especially careful to control our facial expressions when trying to hide our feelings. But most of us are less aware of the ways we move our hands, legs, and feet. Because of this, these movements are better indicators of how we truly feel. It's possible to observe anger by looking beyond the smile and noticing the whitened knuckles and clenched fists. People may talk about how open and honest they want to be, but their real message may come through the gestures of talking from behind a hand or crossing their arms across their chest. Movements such as stroking or combing the hair, glancing in a mirror, or rearranging clothing are called *preening behaviors* and are often signals of sexual interest in another person. There are also *lies of omission* in gestures. This is shown by the person who tells you he's happy or excited while sitting motionless with hands, arms, legs, and posture signaling boredom, discomfort, or fatigue.

UNDERSTANDING OTHERS THROUGH FACIAL EXPRESSIONS

The face and eyes are probably the most noticed parts of the body but are the hardest to read for a number of reasons. First, it's hard to describe the number and kind of expressions we use. Also, facial expressions change very quickly, some fleeting across the face in a fifth of a second. However, you can still pick up messages by watching faces. Look for expressions that seem to be overdone. Often when someone is trying to fool himself or another, he'll emphasize his mask to a point where it seems to be too exaggerated to be true. Another way to detect a person's feelings is to watch his expression at moments when he isn't likely to be thinking about his appearance. Finally, you can watch for *contradictory* expressions on *different* parts of someone's face. His eyes say one thing, but the expression of his mouth or eyebrows may be sending a conflicting message.

The eyes themselves can send several kinds of messages. Meeting someone's glance with your eyes is usually a sign of *involvement,* while looking away signals a desire to *avoid contact*. This is why solicitors on the street try to catch your eye. Once they've made contact, it's harder for the approached person to draw away. The eyes communicate a positive or negative attitude; also dominance or submission. We've all played the game of trying to stare someone down, and in real life there are times when downcast eyes are a sign of giving in.

Even the pupils of our eyes communicate. A person's pupils grow larger in proportion to the degree of interest they have in an object. Thus a good salesman can *increase his profits* by being aware of pupil dilation.

PARALANGUAGE—WHAT ARE WE REALLY SAYING?

The voice itself is another channel of nonverbal communication. It's not the words but how we say them. By changing the word emphasis, we can change the entire meaning of what is being said.

There are a number of other ways our voice communicates: through its tone, speed, pitch, number and length of pauses, volume, and disfluencies (such as stammering, the use of *uh, um, er,* and so on). All these factors together are called *paralanguage,* and they can do a great deal to *reinforce* or *contradict* the message our words convey. Communication through paralanguage isn't always intentional. Often our voices give us away when we're trying to create an impression different from our actual feelings. For example, you've probably had the experience of trying to sound calm and serene when you were really exploding with inner nervousness. Maybe your deception went along perfectly for a while—just the right smile, no telltale fidgeting of the hands, posture appearing relaxed—and then, without being able to do a thing about it, right in the middle of your relaxed comments, your voice squeaked and the charade was over. The point here is to be conscious of our paralanguage, which reinforces or contradicts our true message.

THE IMPORTANCE OF TOUCH

Touching, in addition to being the earliest means we have of making contact with others, is also essential to our healthy development. Touch plays a crucial part in expressing encouragement or tenderness, showing support or praise, as well as many other things. It seems that the more self-confidence a person has, and the better his self-image, the more likely he is to reach out to others.

People are more likely to touch when they give information, give an order, ask a favor, try to persuade, engage in deep conversation, communicate excitement, or receive messages of worry and concern. Touch may be of a functional-professional nature (the intent is nonpersonal, businesslike, and task-oriented); or it may be socially polite, as in the handshake; it may be friendship and warmth (this shows liking and recognizing the other's uniqueness); or it may be love and intimacy, which shows emotional attachment.

Recent research indicates that there is a feeling among many people that an element of warmth is missing from their lives, which they want to recapture. The belief is growing that as we become a more technologically structured society, we also suffer from a kind of emotional *marasmus*—a wasting away of the intense feelings of love, anger, friendship, and fear. Since studies show that physical contact is essential for healthy development, we may find the society we live in begin to place more importance on touching.

REMEMBER, HOW YOU LOOK IS A FORM OF COMMUNICATION

Another way of advertising yourself to others is through your attire. Choice of clothing communicates some definite information about the person living in them. Sometimes people relate to you prompted only by the clothes you wear. And remember that for most it is a common experience that when you look good, you feel good. Proper attire and grooming affect your attitude and behavior.

Many books and articles have been written on how to dress, but generally speaking, in most professions, conservative styles, colors, and patterns will win out over whatever the latest fashion magazines are suggesting for the season. Conservatism in dress conveys to others that you have the situation in control and that you are not easily influenced by others. It is true that the person inside the clothes is more important than the clothes themselves, but remember, how you *look* when you say anything is more important than *what* you say.

BODY TYPES INFLUENCE PERSONALITY CHARACTERISTICS

Now what about the person *inside* of those clothes? For quite some time researchers have been attempting to establish a correlation between body types and certain personality characteristics. There are three main categories of body types. The first is *endomorph*. These people are soft, round, tend to be overweight, and are perceived as more talkative, good-natured, agreeable, and trusting. The second category is *mesomorph*. These people are bony, muscular, athletic, and are perceived as being more adventurous, good-looking, mature, and self-reliant. The third category is *ectomorph*. You would describe these people as being tall, thin, and fragile, and they are perceived as being more tense, nervous, pessimistic, difficult, and quiet.

Keep in mind that these are broad definitions and that personality characteristics are not always associated with the body types as they are listed. Body types occur in a large number of combinations of the three basic categories. Shapes and sizes are controlled, to varying degrees, by heredity, diet, or level of physical activity. However, there is a sufficient level of confidence in the accuracy of the findings to warrant some serious thought. It is true that the physique constitutes only a *partial* statement of who and what you are, but nonetheless, it *is* a nonverbal message that can be especially significant when it is a *first impression*. People who manage to stay in good physical condition present a favorable initial impression. They appear to others as being disciplined and able to take command of any business or personal encounter.

If you are not in the shape you would like to be, regular attention to proper nutrition and vigorous exercise should remedy the situation. As we said, when you look good, you feel good. This is especially true of your physical condition.

Other body aspects also come into play when first impressions are formed. Your choice of cologne or perfume has a great influence on how people react to your presence. Careful selection and application of these products can enhance your position with your business associates. They will notice that you are wearing something unique that sets you apart from others when they come in contact with you during the workday.

Personal habits that involve offensive odors always carry over into the work environment. If you are a cigar, pipe, or cigarette smoker, or enjoy eating onions and garlic, you might want to be aware of how these habits affect the people with whom you interact. If you have ever worked with someone with bad breath or offensive body odor, you know exactly what nonverbal communication really is!

TEN POINTS TO REMEMBER

As we draw this discussion of body signals of the super persuader to a close, there are some points to reemphasize. First, in a normal two-person conversation, 7% of the impact results from *what* people say, 38% from *how* they say it, and 55% from *how they look* while saying it. This may have been previously hard for you to believe, but now you know how many channels of nonverbal communication there are: distance, touch, body posture and tension, facial expression, hand and body movement, dress, physique, tone of voice, speed of speech, as well as disfluencies of speech. These are the ten ways to make your body say what it means.

You should now understand the importance of *congruency* —the matching of your verbal and nonverbal expressions. *Contradicting messages* from two channels are a pretty good indicator of deliberate or unconscious deception, and matching signals *reinforce* your messages. This new awareness of the messages you and others send will help you understand and improve your ability to persuade and communicate with others.

FIVE ACTION STEPS
TO PERSUADE OTHERS
THROUGH YOUR BODY SIGNALS

1. The most useful and effective form of body language is your smile. A genuine smile implies sincerity—and that is usually associated with a willingness to be fair and equitable.

2. Handshakes transmit your self-image. A person with high self-esteem has a firm, confident handshake, while someone who suffers from an inferiority complex will reflect that condition. Let handshaking work to your advantage by doing it with firmness, directness, and conviction, while maintaining direct eye contact.

3. The most convincing body position to show *invulnerability* is to be open and vulnerable. Extend your arms out, with your shoulders back rather than hunched. Expand your body into more space rather than trying to shrink it and withdraw within yourself.

4. In your speech, make use of the "pregnant pause." Don't fear silence when you are thinking of the right words to say to give birth to a new idea. Stop—move—look pensive. All of this communicates that your next idea is very important, even when you're not sure what it's going to be!

5. Maintain congruency between the words you say and what your body is communicating. In this way you are establishing trust and conviction in your ideas as you communicate with self-confidence.

Chapter 4
HOW THE SUPER PERSUADER ESTABLISHES TRUST AND CREDIBILITY

For several years Charles Schultz has celebrated the beginning of football season with a Peanuts story featuring Charlie Brown's troubles with Lucy. The plot is always the same. Lucy offers to hold a football so Charlie Brown can practice his placekicking. But each year she jerks the ball away just as Charlie kicks through, causing him to fall to the ground. We readers always know what will happen. The only suspense involves what Lucy will do or say to overcome Charlie Brown's well-founded suspicions that this year will only be a repetition of the last. For example, one year Lucy explained, "I represent an organization and I'm holding this ball as a representative of that organization." Charlie reasoned that if she represents an organization, she must be sincere, and so he came running full speed to kick the ball. Seconds later, as Charlie lay dazed from the impact of hitting the turf, Lucy explained, "This year's football was pulled away from you through the courtesy of women's lib!"

Most people find Charlie Brown's troubles similar to their own. And in this case the problem involves trust. Should Charlie *trust* Lucy? How could he determine, before he committed himself to a forceful kick at the pigskin, whether he would score a field goal or end up on his back suffering from her taunts? Few of us have to worry about girls offering to hold our footballs when we are out for a little kicking practice, but all of us have to make hard decisions about whether, and how much, and with what, to trust other people.

ESSENTIAL CHARACTERISTICS OF TRUST

Let's begin by considering the context of trust. Trust occurs only in relationships having certain characteristics. The first is *contingency*. This describes situations in which the trusted person's behavior affects the outcomes of the trusting person —in important ways. So there must be a willingness on the part of the trusting person to be vulnerable.

The second condition is *predictability*. This describes situations in which the trusting person has some degree of confidence in his expectations or predictions of the trusted person's behaviors and/or intentions. Without predictability, *hope* may be present, but not trust. Consider a man carrying a large amount of money late at night through a section of town that is known for its high crime rate. If he hears footsteps in the shadows both ahead and behind him, he may *hope* for the best. However, he would have a much different experience if he knows who is there and can predict their behavior by trusting them not to rob him.

The third condition is *alternative options*. This describes situations in which the trusting person can do something other than trust, in which he has a choice whether to *maintain* or *increase* his vulnerability to the other person. And so, when a person is in a situation in which what happens to him is contingent on the behavior of the other, he has some basis for predicting how the other will behave, and he has the option to behave in a way that will *increase* or *limit* the extent to which the other's behavior will affect him; only then will trust occur.

Trusting behaviors are those that *deliberately increase* a person's *vulnerability* to another person. To attain a cognitive state of trust requires that the trusted person be perceived as both *competent* and *well-intentioned*. Competence involves seeing the other's knowledge, judgment, and abilities as adequate. If you broke your leg, you probably would not *trust* your friend to set it for you. You may have no doubts about his good *intentions,* but you might prefer to wait for a doctor and rely on his more competent abilities. On the other hand, there are situations where people are known to be *competent,* but they are not *trusted* because they are not thought to be well-intentioned. Some public officials have this problem.

DEALING WITH THREE BASIC PERSONALITY TYPES

Problems in communication often arise simply because people perceive and convey information differently. There are three basic, and very different, styles of communicating. The quickest way to establish trust and rapport with anyone is first to identify the type of communicator you're dealing with. Let's take a look at the types of people who tend to use each style, and some suggestions that will help you avoid misunderstandings.

The first is *analytical*. Analyzers may be difficult to get to know because they are highly articulate people who express themselves in complicated sentences and analytical terms. They can be very adept at transmitting concepts and ideas. To establish trust very quickly with analyzers, just state the facts and get to the point quickly. They grasp ideas *instantly* and get bored and turned off with long explanations. Moreover, they respect people who speak accurately, know the details, and are organized.

The second type of communicator is *emotional*. Unlike analyzers, who use phrases such as "I think" and "I understand," emotional people express themselves by saying, "This feels right" or "I sense that this is a good thing." Because they operate on such a gut level, they may have trouble putting their feelings into words. When dealing with emotional types, be patient, supply lots of details, and allow them plenty of time to express their ideas. Encourage their feedback, and be liberal with your positive reinforcement.

The third type of communicator is *visual*. These types are good organizers, with a tendency toward perfectionism. Visual people often use expressions such as, "I get the picture" or "I see what you mean" or perhaps, "Look at this." Your best approach with visualizers is to provide them with the overall picture of something, using descriptive phrases and, if possible, visual aids.

ASKING QUESTIONS BUILDS TRUST AND CREDIBILITY

No matter what type of communicator you're talking with, there is an easy way to get them to start talking to you, and that is by asking questions.

Ask questions that appeal to the other person's *interest*, such as, "I hear you're quite a football fan. I missed last Sunday's game, but I hear that the Cowboys looked pretty good. Did you see any of the action on TV?"

Ask questions that lead into discussing a hobby: "I see you're using a brand-new lens. Are you a photography buff like me?"

Ask questions that will prompt others into talk about their jobs: "I see from the parking decal on your car that you're with XYZ Corporation. Are you in the production or engineering end of the company?"

Ask questions that in some way deliver a compliment: "I like your sport coat. May I ask where you bought it? I've been looking for a good clothing store."

Don't ask questions that pry into someone's personal life. Obviously your instincts will warn you not to ask a direct question, such as, "How can you manage the financial strain with two kids in college?" It's only common sense to wait until the other person first signals a willingness to talk by making a comment such as, "Am I glad I planned for the kids' education." This remark is a door opener, and it leaves you free to reply, "I've got two kids in grade school now, and so I have to start planning for their college education. But I'm not sure how. How did you do it?"

When there are only two of you present, asking questions is a great starter toward building trust. When you're with a *group*, you'll have more success using a broader-based technique. Pick a topic that interests as many of the others as possible, and spark a discussion on that topic. Three of the easiest ways to do this are to (1) get them to work together on solving a problem, (2) discuss a hobby or interest that the group has in common, and (3) talk about a spectator experience you've shared together. As you can clearly see, it's easy to get group conversations started simply by getting others talking about a topic everyone finds interesting. All you have to do is speak long enough to get the conversation under way. You can then sit back, listen, and let the others do the talking. Use this approach for a while, and it soon will become instinctive. More importantly, people will quickly realize that when you're around, good conversations start. You'll be welcomed wherever you go.

RESPOND INSTEAD OF REACT

It's almost uncanny the way people spot how you feel about them and how they react to your feelings. Show friendliness and they'll return it, but take a dislike to someone and they'll immediately dislike you in return. That's why people who establish trust and credibility *quickly* always have a positive attitude toward other people. They know that their positive attitude will be spotted and returned in kind. These people unconsciously use some basic techniques to assure their popularity.

Unless you're a hermit, there's no way to avoid contacting other people every day. The way that you *handle* these contacts is the key to whether or not you enjoy them. Unfortunately, here's one all too common way we handle contact with others: We bury our thoughts and feelings deep inside ourselves, put on a smile, and act pleasant. Next, we get together with others who also hide within themselves. Then everyone stands at a safe distance from one other and bounces meaningless words off each others' shells. *Some* people call this communication—I call it drapery talk, and a waste of time. It's like eating the peel and throwing away the banana.

Here's a more rewarding approach: Don't just bounce words around but *respond* to everyone's uniqueness as a person. The easiest way to do this is by giving others your full attention by putting their feelings and thoughts ahead of your own. Do this for a while and you'll soon automatically ask yourself questions such as, "What kind of personality does he have? Is he confident or hesitant, reserved or outgoing? What's his general attitude—is he an optimist or a pessimist, liberal or conservative? When a new idea comes into the conversation, is his first reaction positive or negative?"

Questions like these will quickly give you workable insights into other people. You'll find it easier to respond and speak to each new person in a way he'll *understand*. More importantly, you'll show through your actions and your words that you recognize and respect each person's *uniqueness*. Do this and he'll respect and like you as a person in return.

When you want to be sure that you'll create a positive impression in the other person's mind, discuss a topic that interests *him*, not one that interests *you*. Another way to guarantee that you'll be accepted is to put his inner needs first and your own second.

Many people have trouble clearly expressing what's on their minds, and you can spot them easily. They'll fumble for words, keep repeating the same thought, act hesitantly, and give you an intuitive feeling that they're having a hard time communicating. When you spot such a person, you can help him by listening creatively, to catch the basic thought he's trying to communicate and then to help him express himself clearly and accurately.

USING THE RIGHT WORDS AT THE RIGHT TIME

Failure to establish trust and credibility is often due to not knowing how to use the right words at the right time. Here are some tips to learn to speak the other person's language.

First, use words that move you forward. These are words that people like to hear. They make others feel good about you, and they tend to make others respond to you. Some of these words are *you, yourself, yours, we, our, ourselves, sorry, promise, please, thank you,* and *excuse me*. There is a major communications company that has made it a corporate rule that all letters going out under its letterhead, regardless of who writes them, cannot be mailed if they contain the word *I*. Therefore the words *you* and *yours* really get a workout. The company knows that whomever it deals with will warm to such personal words. These words are always attention-getting; the moment you say them, the people you are talking to become more alert and more responsive.

Second, drop the words that *hold you back*. When people hear these words, they tend to turn away from you, even though they may not understand why they do. Holding-back words are *I, me, myself, my, later,* and *maybe*. Those words usually indicate that you are communicating on your own terms, not on the other person's. The big difference here is point of view. Speaking the other person's language means seeing things from their perspective—that's what *they* like and that's what *they* appreciate. This doesn't mean that you give in to others' demands, or give up your convictions or sell out. But it does mean that by your words you are putting yourself in their shoes, under their hat, and seeing through their eyes.

Third, use *simple words*. This doesn't mean that everything you say has to be one syllable, but get rid of the tongue twisters and the hard-to-understand words if they aren't in the other person's vocabulary. No one knew this better than Winston Churchill. When he needed to rally the British to their country's defense, he didn't give them double-talk. Instead, he told them in words they understood, "I have nothing to offer but blood, toil, tears and sweat." Churchill shared what he had learned when he wrote, "All my life I have earned my living by words that I write and words that I speak. If I have learned about the use of words, what I know best and what counts most is this: of all the words I know, the short words are of most use. They are the words others know. They are the words that *bring* other men to know. And they are the words which move men."

You cannot establish trust and credibility if you need an interpreter. Consider this memo that an insurance adjuster sent to the main office: "The pressure involved in getting depositions from on-site witnesses for both the claimant and the disputing party has made it necessary to revise the suspense date set for arbitration of the findings upwards of three days with no slippage foreseen." The translation is, "The full report will be on your desk Thursday." Remember the rule to keep it simple—KISS. Along with that, fit your words to the occasion. Depending on the customer, car salesmen know whether they should talk about style, comfort, beauty, and safety, or horsepower and compression ratios. When you're with a doctor, don't try to impress with some big words you read in a medical book. Explain that you have a stomachache, and where it hurts when you breathe. The doctor will understand, and it's very doubtful that the advice will be "to take ten grains of the acetyl derivative of salicylic acid and retire." Rather, you'll hear, "Take two aspirin and go to bed."

The fourth point is *not to wave red-flag words*. These are words that arouse the other person's defenses. These words would be the ones that oppose his belief systems in the areas of religion, politics, race and ethnic background, family, and economics. The key is to get to know the person and then avoid the words that you sense would rub him the wrong way. This will not be a problem when you are communicating with someone who shares your beliefs (obviously an enlightened being!). The trouble occurs when you are discussing an issue with one whose views are *opposing*. Again, this does not mean that you should sell out your principles or not discuss a particular subject. Just use discretion in choosing your words, and allow there to be a difference of ideas.

The fifth point is to *go easy on the slang*. There's nothing wrong with slang. Strong slang expressions can often be valuable in making a specific point. However, they tend to date quickly and to be replaced by newer words or phrases, and certain slang expressions will carry political, emotional, or generational associations you might not wish to convey. They rarely serve you as well as the straightforward expression. "Crash in my pad" may be colorful, and perhaps the other person knows exactly what you mean. But you'll communicate better with, "Why not stay over at my place?" Also, use foreign expressions sparingly, and only if you really know what they mean, so that when you do use them, they will work to your advantage.

The sixth point is to *say what you mean*. Don't use weasel words or loophole words or words that sound like one thing but really mean something else. The only place for squirm-out words is in disclaimers. For example, say, "Let's have lunch together on Tuesday if it's convenient" but not, "Why don't we get together for lunch sometime?" The first says exactly what you mean, lunch together on Tuesday. The second almost says, "I really don't care if we eat together or not." Think of the times you've been startled by someone who has missed an appointment or stood you up and then said, "But I thought you meant . . ." Next time, say what you mean.

The seventh point is to *mean what you say*. One way to really mess up your credibility is to have no intention of doing what you say you'll do, or going where you'll say you'll go. Have you ever had someone say, "I'll give you a call" and in the back of your mind you ask yourself, "Should I wait to hear from you?" Words like these belong to the people who are all talk and no action. You may be tempted to use them because you know they are words that won't let people pin you down. They are words and phrases such as, *perhaps, we'll see, sometime, let me think about it, I'll try to get around to it*— and there are hundreds more. The point is, if you want to be credible and trustworthy, you also *want* to be pinned down and dependable. You want people to know that your word stands for something, that you can be counted on. If you don't mean what you say, don't say it at all.

The last point is to forget the profanity. The person who notices your profanity and resents it, or is offended by it, is often a person who uses it to excess and doesn't realize the image he or she is projecting. Don't be tempted to be like that person. Stand out by being different. Ira Hayes, a very prominent executive and outstanding public speaker, has this to say about profanity: "You cheapen yourself when you use profanity. It isn't needed; it can't help you—so why do it?"

RISING ABOVE SHYNESS AND TIMIDITY

All through their lives many people fail to live up to their full potential as communicators. In fact, they actually hold themselves down—not because they lack ability but simply because they lack faith in themselves. Self-confidence is the secret to establishing trust and credibility. The way in which you think about yourself and the amount of belief you have in yourself sets the whole tone as to how much others can believe in you. Whenever you see someone holding himself down, you can be sure that his way of thinking is his own worst enemy. There's no need for this. Anyone can turn his thinking in the right direction. There are techniques that anyone can use to rise above common hang-ups that prevent him from extending himself to others and gaining their trust.

To rise above timidity, one must stop fearing the unknown. There's no way anyone can escape from facing unfamiliar situations. Life moves so fast today, it's impossible to live normally without running into new problems. So why not just accept the fact that you have to face new and different situations every day? Then, when you face an unknown, think *objectively* about the problem, and not *subjectively* about yourself.

"TURNAROUND THINKING" PRODUCES POSITIVE RESULTS

Many people are bashful and self-conscious. But they don't let it get the best of them because they have learned *turn-around thinking*. They simply turn their thoughts 180 degrees away from themselves. They don't worry about how other people may react to what they say and do; instead, they think only about other people—what they're interested in, what *they* enjoy talking about. Soon they become so engrossed in the conversation that they completely forget their shyness.

Some people are like ostriches—they poke their heads in the sand whenever they face a forceful personality. This is easy to overcome. First, accept the fact that you have weaknesses, then realize that it's uncomfortable when you're surrounded by others who are strong where you're weak. At the same time, accept the fact that you have strengths as well as weaknesses. Everyone has his own uniqueness. Accept these two simple facts and you'll clearly see that there's no logical reason to feel inferior. When you feel yourself being overawed by a strong personality, turn off your emotions and turn on your logic. Simply remember that you are a perfectly normal person with strengths and weaknesses, and so is he.

The play-it-safe person says little and carefully measures every word. You can't go through life playing it safe—it robs you of all your excitement and interest. A free-flowing graciousness and an honest interest in people will certainly help you advance faster than a play-it-safe attitude. Allow your enthusiasm to sparkle through as you show genuine interest and concern for others. They will reward you with their trust in your credibility.

FIVE ACTION STEPS TO ESTABLISH TRUST AND CREDIBILITY

1. Identify the type of communicator you're talking with, and design your language to what he will most easily understand and accept. Subtly match that person's posture, energy level, and eye contact.

2. Show that you understand the other person's point of view. Express empathy in saying, "I understand how you feel."

3. Ask for clarification if you feel there are discrepancies in communication. Do it in a non-threatening way, such as by saying, "I want to be sure I understand you. What I hear you saying is . . ."

4. Realize that trust cannot be forced. Sometimes it is helpful to discover reasons *why* the other person does not trust. Previous negative experiences may be keeping them from extending trust to *you*.

5. Trusting behavior on your part may produce trust being extended by the other person. Extend

friendliness, warmth, sincere interest in their problems, and they will not doubt your credibility when you are extending help to them.

As you begin to use the techniques we've shared with you in this chapter, you will find that the level of trust and credibility extended to you by others will increase day by day. You'll be identified as a person who is a sincere, honest, capable communicator. One who *deserves* trust and credibility. This is an essential quality of the Super Persuader.

Chapter 5
HOW THE SUPER PERSUADER USES PERSONAL POWER

There's a saying that goes like this, "You will get treated in life the way you train people to treat you." When you speak the language of power, you will get respect and courtesy. You will take control of conversations, and you will be a leader. A person of power is a person who is recognized. He or she is someone who walks tall and is not lightly dismissed. He or she is someone who demands fair treatment regardless of the situation. And he or she is a person of value with special skills, knowledge, authority, or some useful quality that is desirable. A person of power is someone people want to know and be associated with.

THE SUBMISSIVE PERSONALITY

People without power have submissive personalities. Their natural tendency is to appease, or submit to others. They are uncertain of the value of their opinions, ideas, skills, and knowledge. Sometimes they devalue these things and consider them to be insignificant. As a result, they present themselves fearfully, seeking approval or respect through modesty, pleasing others, and always being in a supportive role.

The end result of being submissive, and hoping that others will recognize your value, is that no one ever does! They won't let you lead, direct, instruct, or negotiate. They won't even let you be an equal partner, unless they're the submissive type, too, and ultimately such a relationship will prove weakening to both.

Most people do not *create* events; they *react* to them. Submissive people are almost totally reactive. They constantly try to please and continually subject their goals to those of others. Therefore they get little of what *they want* and *need* for themselves. Submissive people often carry around a great deal of hidden anger.

THE CREATIVE DOMINANT PERSONALITY

The opposite of a reactive person is the *creator*. These people see things as opportunities for creativity and problem solving. They go through life imagining possibilities, setting goals, and causing events to happen. They tend to create the situations to which reactive people respond.

The entrepreneurs, the scientists, the leaders in business, the innovators, are all creative, dominant personalities. To become more of this type of a person may be your goal. In this direction lies the freedom, excitement, creative satisfaction, and financial reward you want in life. This is the way to become the center of a world that is largely your own creation, where you will find yourself surrounded by people *you* want to know and who will listen to you and respect you. Also, you will reap many other benefits. You'll discover that conversation is more enjoyable when others pay attention to you, when interruptions are greatly reduced, and when people care about your views and opinions. You will clarify the nature of your relationship with those close to you. Promotions will come your way faster, and you'll find your work becomes much easier when you learn how to delegate to subordinates. You'll understand people better, and you'll soon have more powerful people as your friends and allies.

A POWER PERSON IS A
SUPER PERSUADER

Power personalities project their opinions with confidence and pursue them with tenacity. If others disagree, their goal is to win them over to their way of thinking. Submissive personalities convey a lack of self-confidence because they are reluctant to possess an opinion that might be wrong. They use words that allow them to test the water with a toe before committing the whole foot. Notice the difference in these examples: A power personality says, "*I* want more time." A submissive person says, "*Most people* would need more time." A power personality says, "*I'll* put *my* department on overtime." A submissive person says, "*Someone* will have to go on overtime." The power people place themselves directly on the line and accept ownership for their opinions.

There are a number of devices in our language that serve as *de-emphasizers*. If you are using any of the following five mannerisms, you are showing yourself to be a *submissive lightweight*.

FIVE MANNERISMS OF A SUBMISSIVE LIGHTWEIGHT

1. The word *should* is a great power word, but *really should* is not. The *really* qualifies the statement and weakens it. When you tell someone that they really should do something, you're also giving them permission not to do it. *Really should* is not a *command* but a way of releasing yourself of the *obligation* to command. *Should* is most powerful when the force behind it remains mysterious. If you say *should* to someone who has the presence of mind to say, "Says who?"—then your bluff has been called. The easiest way to enforce a *should* is to find a *should* category that pushes the other person's fear button. Examples are fear of mother, God, social opinion, or losing money.

2. A *tag question* is a statement with a question tagged onto the end. "It's a nice day, *isn't it?*" There are times when the tag question can be useful. Tag questions are sometimes practical conversational tools because they serve to get conversations going or to get information about which you're uncertain ("The party's from five to nine, isn't it?"). A power person may use a tag question to elicit information without revealing that he doesn't know. "The president fired John, didn't he?" Tag questions can also become heavy threats. "That's not the way you mean to be talking to me, is it?" Or in an emphatic way, "I think this is the *last* time we're going to let them get away with that nonsense, isn't it?"

   But there's a dark side to tag questions; they can weaken any statement. For instance: "That's a great movie, isn't it?"; "The President's turning out to be a good leader, isn't he?"; "I really should quit my job, shouldn't I?"; "This wine is very good, don't you agree?" These tag questions say, "You are wiser or otherwise better than I am, so I'm putting myself forth for you either to approve or disapprove. If you reject my statements, I'll take them back at once and go along with you. Just don't reject me."

3. *Qualifiers* can also be statement softeners, but while tag questions work by questioning the statement, qualifiers equivocate. Classic qualifiers are *somewhat, sort of, well, perhaps, kind of, a little, I wonder,* and *rather* (as in "a rather nice house").

The addition of a qualifier weakens a statement of opinion. It softens the potential conflict with the other person. And it prepares the way for a graceful retreat. Listen to these power statements, followed by qualified statements:

> I don't want to. [I don't really want to.]
>
> I don't think that's a good idea. [Well, I don't think it's a good idea.]
>
> That's incorrect. [That's more or less incorrect.]
>
> Is that a good idea? [I wonder if that's a good idea.]
>
> I like it. [I kind of like it.]
>
> I'm sure. [I'm pretty sure.]
>
> You're right. [You're probably right.]

4. Another form of statement softener is the *disclaimer*. The disclaimer asks forgiveness for what you're about to say. Here are a few different types:

> I don't want you to get mad, but . . .
>
> This may sound crazy, but . . .

I'm not entirely certain, but . . .

I could be mistaken but . . .

Disclaimers are a way of hedging. You don't want to be held responsible for your statement, and therefore you hedge to avoid being diminished in the other's eyes. So you use a disclaimer when you anticipate that another person is going to take issue with what you're about to say. When you use a disclaimer, you're telling the other person that you know what you're about to say won't sound right, but you want to proceed, anyway, and would like to be heard out sympathetically.

In most cases, disclaimers are ridiculous. You think you are preparing for fair-minded judgment, but in fact you're signaling the other person that you are feeling very submissive, and you are giving advance notice that your statement can be used against you.

Power people rarely need special dispensations from listeners. They're strong enough to look the other person straight in the eyes and say what's on their minds, relying on authority and charisma to support them and to hold objections at bay.

5. *Pause words* and *phrases,* such as *er, um, you know, like, it occurred to me that,* and *well* are all space fillers. At times they serve a valuable purpose. But more often, fillers make you look slow, dull-witted, and confused. So use fillers only when you need to slow things down for a particular effect. For submissive people, fillers become a nervous habit. Have you ever heard anyone who used *you know* after every sentence? You may have found this amusing, but you probably felt annoyed and concluded that the person was semiliterate.

LANGUAGE OF THE SUPER PERSUADER

Another aspect of communication that separates power people from submissive people is the language they use. This separation occurs because words have hidden meanings and special connotations that go beyond their definitions. For instance, the words *luxurious, elegant, plush,* and *extravagant* have similar meanings. But do they really? Luxurious has a sensuous quality to it. A movie star may have a luxurious home. *Elegant* indicates wealth. A proper Bostonian might have an elegant home. *Plush* might describe the home of a janitor turned million-dollar lottery winner. *Extravagant* makes you think of someone who goes overboard. So power people carefully choose their words to create impressions and thus gain ascendancy and lend force to their communications.

When words of high finance are applied to your personal financial situation, you can increase your status, imply greater wealth, and downplay your money problems. Listen to the difference: A submissive person, talking about the actual situation would say, "I'm broke." A power person, using high-finance words, says, "I'm experiencing negative cash flow." Would you rather say, "I'm deeply in debt" or "I'm very well leveraged?" Here's another example: "Everything I've got in the world is in my checking and savings accounts" or, "My assets are handled by my banker." Both examples represent the same situation, but the *choice* of the *right phrases* for the *right audience* can convey force, authority, and leadership.

IT'S HOW YOU SAY IT THAT COUNTS

Now we're going to consider ways that you can improve the delivery of these power words. There are a number of benefits you will gain from learning new ways to use your voice and body. With *power words* you give off an air of command and assurance. With *submissive words* you appear timid, as if you're used to taking orders rather than giving them. It's impossible, however, to use the power words effectively if you are still using the voice and body position of a submissive person. Your delivery style makes an enormous impact on whether or not your directions are clearly understood. It also helps in getting ideas and projects *accepted*. In power struggles, your body language and delivery can be used deliberately to add emphasis, to put your opponents off-guard, and to intensify meanings without committing yourself to them.

The nonverbal aspects of using power words can be easy to learn if you think of yourself as an actor playing the role of a very powerful person. This can make it easier for you to let go of submissive thoughts and actions that have been holding you back.

Research studies have shown that people attach certain vocal characteristics to various character qualities. Based on these alone, people make judgments about personalities, morals, social status, and so on. Using this research, we can define *power people qualities* and *submissive vocal qualities* quite easily.

The sound of authority is slightly loud but relaxed. Power people project their voice so that people far away from them can still hear, even when what they're saying is in a whisper. Projection isn't hard to learn. You simply increase the loudness of your voice without changing the pitch or quality. Normally you speak higher and more harshly when you shout. Submissive people speak either too soft or too loud. The soft voice is because they're afraid to be authoritative. The too loud voice is also due to insecurity; it's an effort to compensate for inferior feelings, probably resulting from years of not being listened to.

Power people keep their voices at an even volume. They save *shouting* as a reaction to extreme threat or intimidation. Occasionally they will speak so softly that their subordinates have to lean forward and maintain absolute silence to hear every word. This is effective when you have built up to a very important point that you want to make.

Pitch is the *level* of your voice. Musically we call human voices soprano, alto, tenor, baritone, and bass. Our culture prefers low-pitched voices for both men and women. A low voice conveys assurance and relaxed authority. We tend to believe that high-pitched voices belong to people who are insecure, immature, or slightly hysterical. *Power people* also don't *vary* the pitch of their voices as much as *submissive people*. They give the impression that they are *always* in control and *never* ruled by emotion. It is possible to *change* the pitch of your voice. This is mostly accomplished through the use of diaphragmatic breathing—use the entire diaphragm when inhaling and exhaling, not just your neck, shoulders, and upper chest.

Although people speak at different speeds in different parts of the country, power people generally speak slightly slower than the average rate of speed in their area. This gives them an aura of seriousness and deliberation. They also tend to speak at a steady speed. Speed shifts are used to deliver specific messages. Slowing down is for a threat or intimidation. Speeding up is to end a meeting or conversation.

Power people use a rhythm of speech that catches attention, and it makes the content memorable. Their speech is smooth-flowing, with deliberate pauses to make key points. Submissive people's talk is jerky, uneven, and inconsistent.

The *body language* of power people indicates their willingness to occupy all the space available, and then some. When sitting or walking, power people stretch out. They walk freely with their shoulders back, their heads up, and their arms swinging. They have a long stride and move briskly. When they are sitting, they are relaxed and use the arms of a chair, or stretch an arm along the back of a sofa, or lean their arms across a desk. As you can guess, submissive people are just the opposite. They seem to apologize for taking up any space at all. They walk with their heads down to avoid eye contact, their shoulders hunched, and have a short stride. When sitting, they keep their arms and legs close to their bodies. Submissive people also avert eye contact, smile frequently and inappropriately, and use many exaggerated facial expressions. This shows their eagerness to please, their fear of offending, and their anxiety about holding someone's attention. Eye contact is important because it's a sign of dominance and a link to holding attention.

Our personalities are complex and unique to each of us. We don't want to clone you into being a specific "power personality"; there isn't any need to do that. There *are* certain traits, however, that are effective in helping other people to perceive you as being a leader.

First of all you must decide firmly to be accepted as a dominant, powerful person. *You* direct the action by thinking up projects and things to do. Present your ideas positively and confidently, and respond to the ideas of others in a way that lets you focus the questions. Issue commands in such a way that people do what you ask, but without resentment. Be precise. Use exact words rather than vague generalities. Be concise. The shorter the statement, the clearer it is, and the stronger you appear. Have a gracious courtesy that never apologizes for yourself or seeks approval. Don't make promises you can't keep, and never offer amends when apologizing for a mistake. Don't brag, but do let others know about your accomplishments. You may use nonverbal clues in the form of props or verbal hints that are too tantalizing to ignore. *Never* put yourself down. This is the worst form of submissiveness. It invites others to take power over you, and advertises shortcomings that may not even be important until *you* mention them.

Power people don't speak to everyone in the same way. All of us are involved simultaneously in many different relationships, power people perhaps more so. Let's take a closer look at these relationships and the kind of power speaking that belongs to each. Complete dominance over everyone is lonely, and the isolation it brings is unnecessary, inappropriate, and destructive. Most of the time—with our friends, family, lovers and colleagues—we want to have peer relationships, a respectful equality that comes from a recognition by two people of *each other's* power. Sometimes we first have to earn their respect. At other times the hand of equality is immediately extended.

CODOMINANT VERSUS THE COSUBMISSIVE RELATIONSHIP

There are two kinds of peer relationships. *Codominance* refers to the relationship between two dominant personalities. They recognize themselves as being equal in power, and live and work in cooperation. They talk to each other in nonaggressive language and use courtesy and deference. They *listen* and *respond* to what each says, trying to anticipate and meet the other's needs. The other kind of peer relationship is *cosubmissive*. This develops when two people who lack power and initiative get together to console each another, complain, and support themselves in self-pity. In their conversations they complain about the injustices of the world and of all those who mistreat them. Instead of actually helping each other, they take turns in supporting the other's fantasies. Cosubmissives are great friends as long as neither tries to change. If you are a submissive person who decides to become a power person, accept the fact that you will be less close to your cosubmissive friends. When you stop talking negatively, you'll begin to replace your cosubmissive friendships with more challenging and rewarding ones.

When changing power balances with loved ones, the most important thing to remember is that the power struggle should not endanger the life of the relationship. Avoid power struggles centered on sensitive topics. Change the power balance through straightforward talking, rather than through games. If you want to be recognized as a power person and you haven't been before, have your friend or lover see you in a new light. Create situations where you are more assertive and decisive, and cease using submissive language.

Love relationships are often power struggles in which the more committed person has the lesser power. As a relationship moves into a long-term commitment, it's very important for the future of any relationship that both parties allow each other centers of power and areas of personal freedom within the relationship.

Business power is a hierarchy. To get power in business, you have to compete successfully and project a power image. Business leaders only promote those who are adaptable, personally and professionally, to high management positions. This means that if you are going to be accepted, you must sound, look, and act right. Which means, be "like them." To get ahead, be positive in your conversations with peers and superiors, but don't presume or push. With those who are your subordinates, be assertive and take command of any projects that could be a source of prestige. Don't force obedience or use cutthroat tactics.

Your overall goal is to be seen as a leader and the best person on your level. Avoid factional conflicts. Acknowledge everyone's concerns. Deal with challenges firmly. Make sure everyone understands their assignment. Present ideas by leading people to believe that it was *their* idea.

We hear and respond to power people on an instinctive level. You are not restricted to being completely dominant or completely submissive. Undoubtably you are dominant in some areas of your life and submissive in others. By using the methods and techniques that we've just covered, you now have the ability to establish relationships you want, in which you and the other person mutually acknowledge and respect each other's rights and powers.

FIVE ACTION STEPS TO TEST AND IMPROVE YOUR PERSONAL POWER

1. When you want someone to do something, do you ask them directly or do you hint around and hope they get the idea? Power people use emphasis in putting themselves directly on the line and asking for exactly what they want.

2. Do you use a lot of qualifying verbal mannerisms, such as, *you know, sort of,* and *maybe*? Power people do not use words that will weaken their opinions or prepare them for defeat.

3. Have you expanded your vocabulary to the point where you can accurately imply subtextual meanings or connotations to that which you describe? Power people carefully *choose* their words to create impressions.

4. Do you say, "I'll pay you out of my next paycheck" or "I've already allocated resources to take care of you"? Power people use words of high finance to convey force, authority, and leadership.

5. Do you talk at a faster rate than average, or do you talk in vague generalities? Power people use short, concise sentences. They talk at a slower speed. And they use precise words.

By using these suggestions, you can become a person who is recognized as a person of value. You will be someone people want to know and be associated with. And you will be able to persuade others through your personal power.

Chapter 6
SUPER PERSUASION THROUGH BETTER LISTENING

Consider the following statement: "I know that you think I understood what you said, but you didn't say what you thought you did, so I have no way of knowing what you want until you know what I thought you meant." What this phrase so aptly demonstrates is that for any conversation to have real meaning, attentive listening is essential. We're now going to take a closer look at how you can make your listening skills even more rewarding and productive.

CLEARING YOUR MIND

There's only one way to listen productively, and that is to remove all distractions from your mind so that you can concentrate on the speaker. Most distractions come directly from your own thoughts, senses, and emotions.

If you took a bottle and filled it with a quart of orange juice, the liquid inside would be pure juice. But if you took the same bottle and filled it with a pint of orange juice and a pint of water, the liquid inside would be neither pure juice nor pure water. Most people do the same sort of thing in conversations—they half fill their minds with the message they're listening to, and half with their *own* thoughts. When they do this, their minds are like the second bottle—it's neither the speaker's message nor their own thoughts, but a mixture of the two. You can correct this common mistake by learning to clear your mind of all personal thoughts and concentrating only on the speaker's words. Mastering this ability is sure to increase your listening productivity tenfold.

Sometimes a great new idea pops into your mind while you are listening to someone else. Often the idea is important and you don't want to lose it. How do you keep the idea in mind and still devote your concentration to the other person? When this happens, a good solution is to interrupt the speaker politely and ask him to bear with you for a few seconds while you write your idea down. Once the idea has been recorded, your mind will once again be free to give total attention to the speaker—and that's something they really appreciate.

Another hindrance to good listening is the annoying habit of second-guessing. Since we are able to think much faster than we can speak, it's often tempting to listen to the other person for a few minutes, then second-guess what point he is leading up to. Second-guessing, when it remains unverbalized, usually only annoys the listener, since it can make following the thread of the speakers conversation difficult. (Keep in mind that your distraction might show in your body language.)

This habit can become plainly insulting, however, if the listener interrupts the speaker and tries to complete the speaker's thought. Although this may be good mental exercise, it's extremely bad for human relations. The other person is certain to leave the conversation with a very low estimate of your sincerity as a listener. Those who are sought after by other people listen attentively and are able to control their own thoughts; only amateurs play the second-guessing game.

MAINTAIN EYE CONTACT

Consider how important communication is to psychologists; it's their main tool for helping people change their behavior. It's only natural, then, that they are always looking for more effective ways to converse. In one recent experiment, psychology students were told to conduct a series of five-minute counseling sessions using various approaches. All sessions were videotaped and analyzed. The major finding was that the best results were obtained when the trainees went out of their way to maintain eye contact. They listened better when they looked directly at the speaker. In everyday discourse, this is an easy thing to do. Maintain eye contact and it can improve your listening productivity tremendously.

In addition to keeping eye contact, your ears should tune in as well. There may be a television set turned on in the room, other people talking loudly enough for you to hear, loud music playing nearby—all of these, and other distracting sounds, can draw your mind away from the speaker's message. You can train yourself to focus your ears, as well as your eyes, on the other person, in order to tune out all other sounds except the speaker's voice. You are at your conversational best when you keep both your eyes and your ears in close contact with the speaker.

LISTEN OBJECTIVELY

It would be natural for you to react emotionally if someone said, "There's something that you do that bothers me, and I refuse to put up with it any longer" or "I know you feel strongly about this, but so do I, and I disagree with you." In both cases the speaker wants to tell you something that's important to him, and in both cases your emotional reaction could prevent you from listening to him. That's why you'll notice that good communicators always keep their emotions under control and make every attempt to listen objectively. They know they can't respond intelligently to what the other person is saying until they know exactly how he *feels*.

At first glance it would seem that controlling your thoughts, senses, and emotions may seem to be time- and effort-consuming, but it really isn't hard. All you have to do is keep aware of the need for control. After a short time it will become second-nature for your mind, senses, and emotions to react automatically to clear themselves of distractions as soon as another person begins to speak. When this process becomes second-nature, it will be easy to concentrate freely on the speaker. You'll do a much better job of hearing what someone has to say. Mastering this ability will not only increase your reputation as a good listener, but will also add greatly to the amount of personal enjoyment you derive from your discussions.

LET THEM KNOW YOU'RE ALIVE!

If there's one person who can annoy almost anyone, it's the blank-faced listener. A classic example is the mother who gives directions or makes a request of her children as they continue to watch TV or play, apparently ignoring her. When she loses her temper and yells, "You haven't heard a word I've said!" they turn very calmly and repeat her sentences verbatim. Sure, these are typical kids, but how often do you run into adults with the same behavior? Think about the people you know. How many of them actually show interest on their faces when you talk with them? You can stare at their deadpan expressions forever and never know for sure if they're listening to you, thinking their own thoughts, or in some cases, if they're even mentally awake.

Now think of the most animated person you know and recall how she reacts in a conversation with you. She makes you feel that she's really interested in you, and she's a real pleasure to talk with. Chances are that the most highly animated person you know is a female, because women are generally more animated than men. But there's absolutely no reason at all why there should be any difference between the sexes on this point. It's easy for *anyone* to be animated once they learn that their face isn't really distorted when they allow their inner feelings to show through. Animation is vital to any meaningful exchange because when someone talks with you, that person can't read your mind, and the only way he or she can tell if you're listening is by your outward actions. The best actions that you can give him are real and revealing facial expressions. Go ahead and use them, even if at first you feel that you're overdoing it. Keep on letting your face reveal your inner feelings; this listening technique will soon become a part of your natural personality. Once you've become an animated listener, you'll be surprised by how it will make you much more welcome in conversational gatherings.

BALANCE GIVING AND TAKING

Giving will also make you a better listener. It's a draining experience to talk to someone who asks you questions and listens to your answers but adds nothing of his own to the conversation. Although everyone realizes that it's bad to monopolize a conversation by constant talking, most people don't understand that it's equally bad not to talk *enough*. Good listening requires more than just giving someone a chance to talk and to express himself. Good listening requires both giving as well as taking. The people who are conversing should exchange opinions and information. Sought-after conversationalists listen and give the other person a chance to express himself but also add information of their own so that the other person will feel that he's getting something out of the conversation too. When you play the role of listener, you should aim for a balance of give-and-take.

It's perfectly all right to base your comments on what the other person says, but rather than repeating his thought, try to add some new facts. For instance, when meeting someone new, a good listener may say, "Hi, I'm Tom Jones. I hear that we're almost neighbors. I live on Friendly Court. Is your home near there?" The good listener has encouraged the speaker to open up and share other information rather than just to respond with his name. The good listener also words his comments in a way that shows that he understands what the other person is saying. By giving information while in a listening role, you help the other person express himself without draining him dry, simply by asking series of questions. Establishing a good balance between listening and talking is one sure way to turn any conversation into a rewarding and fulfilling one for everyone involved.

DON'T LET WORDS
GET IN THE WAY

Many times the *words* another person says do not express the real message he wants to convey. Even though he's not saying what he means, he still expects you to hear and react to his true thoughts. Sounds like an impossible situation, but it happens every day. As an example, two friends may be talking, and one is telling the other how her old dresses don't fit anymore. She says, "For two weeks I've been going from store to store, but the stores are either out of the smaller sizes, or the dresses don't flatter my new figure." What she is really saying is, "I am proud that I lost ten pounds, and now my old clothes don't fit anymore." If the friend would listen carefully, she could win favor and friendship by congratulating the weight loss. If she were not a good listener, she may have responded with a complaint about her bad shopping experiences and would have annoyed her friend. This kind of subtlety is a common human trait because many people think it bad manners to compliment themselves directly.

Similarly, many people don't like to criticize another person directly. So rather than say what they're thinking, they make up a white lie. This practice is so natural and universal that advertising professionals often base ads on it. For example, one ad I've seen shows Tom, a nice guy but with a personal-appearance problem that repels others. The first scene shows a pretty woman turning him down for a date. But rather than giving the real reason, she says that she's busy on Tuesday night. Tom doesn't listen carefully enough to catch the fact that she isn't saying what's really on her mind—that she doesn't want to date him because she's turned off by his personal appearance. Scene two has the office blabbermouth talking to Tom and accidentally referring to his problem. Tom then uses the advertised product. The final scene shows Tom at dinner with the pretty woman. But rather than saying, "You really look nice now that your problem is solved," she says, "You look great. Have you been on vacation?" Again the girl uses a subtle subtext and doesn't really say what she's thinking.

The commercial is exaggerated, but it does illustrate a conventional truth. Many people don't listen carefully enough to catch whether or not someone is really saying what's on his mind. Good listeners have learned these two tricks that help them listen between the lines and spot subtlety. First of all, *be alert*. Often we don't hear the real message because we're more interested in talking about ourselves than in listening to what the other person wanted to say. Trick number two is to *look for patterns*. Once you're alert and listening attentively, you'll be much more likely to spot those times when someone isn't saying what he's thinking. In the TV commercial, an alert Tom wouldn't have needed a water-fountain blabbermouth to cue him in on his problem; he would have searched for patterns in the way people reacted whenever he was near them.

Patterns can take many forms. For instance, when a specific topic is being discussed, if someone pulls away from you ever so slightly, it is a surefire hint that your opinion on that subject conflicts with his. He can also subtly warn you by raising his voice or by speaking a little faster in a somewhat nervous voice. Whatever form the pattern takes, an alert listener finds it easy to listen between the lines, to spot the pattern and analyze it, and then to reply to the real communication. This is the secret that many good conversationalists have used to establish their reputations as good listeners. It's an easy and natural secret to use, and there is no reason why you cannot use it too.

A SINCERE PERSON IS A PERSUASIVE PERSON

Of all the personality traits, the one that drives people away most quickly is insincerity. Luckily nearly everyone is sincere at heart, but even the most sincere person can listen in such a poor way that he gives the *appearance* of being insincere. Let's take a look at four examples.

Consider this episode: You're having lunch with your friend Sam, and he expresses an interest in your woodworking hobby, saying that he's always wanted to make a piece of furniture but didn't know how to go about it. He asks you for some hints. Naturally you're proud of your talents and are glad to answer Sam's questions. You start by explaining the importance of choosing the right wood, then you go over the process of joining each piece, and finally you describe how to sand, stain, and seal each piece so that it matches. When you stop, Sam asks why it's so important to choose the right wood. What gave Sam the appearance of insincerity was the timing of his question. He should have asked it at the most logical time—early in the conversation when you first stressed the importance of choosing the right wood. His poor timing was caused either by slow thinking or a desire not to interrupt. But whatever the cause, he damaged his friendship with you by creating the impression of being an insincere listener.

Example number two involves your neighbor Charlie. He's having trouble with his yard turning brown at the first sign of the summer heat. Knowing that you had the same problem, he asks you for your advice. So you drop what you're doing, go over to his house, and show him that the bottom layer of his lawn is a mat of dead grass, deep roots, and peat moss. You explain how the new grass dries up and dies once the weather turns warm, and that a landscaper once advised you to rotary-till your own lawn to solve a similar problem. Since you did that, you no longer have a problem. Charlie realizes that it's a big project and asks if there are any alternatives. You explain that there are chemicals, but they take years to be effective, and rotary-tilling is really the only option. He agrees that this is probably the best action for him to take and notes again the successful outcome that you've had. You go back home feeling good for helping out, even though you did lose an hour out of a very busy Saturday. The next day you see Charlie throwing grass seed right out over the old, dried-out mat. Perhaps Charlie's appearance of insincerity came about because he wasn't convinced by what you said. He's under no obligation to follow your advice, but he does have a responsibility to be honest and sincere. If Charlie disagrees with you, he could thank you for your advice and admit that you're probably right, but it's too much work and expense. Though you may be disappointed in his decision, you would respect him for his honesty and straightforward sincerity. Or it may be that he agreed with you at first, then changed his mind after thinking about the time and expense involved. That's all right too. But he did ask for your advice, and you went out of your way to give it. Therefore he does owe you a thanks and an explanation of some kind, even if he's changed his mind. What caused Charlie's appearance of insincerity was false agreement—he told you one thing and did another.

The third example has you talking with an acquaintance, Mary, who attended the same social event you did last night.

You remark on how good the food was, how much you enjoyed the host's graciousness, especially in planning such clever icebreaker games so that everyone could have a chance to get to know each other better. Mary agrees that she also had a very good time. You leave the conversation feeling good about Mary because she thinks the same way you do. Later you meet Jeff, who has also discussed the party with Mary. Jeff tells how Mary had said she disliked the party; she'd told him the host was a bore and that games are for kids. Mary was more than just insincere—she was outright dishonest. Throughout your conversation she agreed with you, then later expressed opposite opinions to someone else. Perhaps she did this because she thinks that the way to make friends is simply to agree with whatever the other person says. Unfortunately dishonest agreement, no matter how well-intentioned the motive, can only result in being thought of as insincere.

The last example has you talking with Susan, who knows that you invest in the stock market. She asks how you're doing, and you reply that you made a 10% profit in one week. She asks how you did it, and you tell her that you use a rather complicated process. She begs you to elaborate. Convinced of her sincerity, you explain your system of finding those few stocks that tend to change in price quickly; then you study their price patterns carefully. When you think a stock is about to go up in price, you quickly buy a few hundred shares and then sell them as soon as they go up two or three points. You keep your explanation simple and use lots of examples. You then ask Susan if she understands, and she says, "Yes. You take a lot of money and invest it for a long time." Such a total lack of attentiveness is insincerity at its worst! Susan's questions, designed to encourage you to talk about one of your interests, were asked only with the aim of making you like *her*, and nothing else. There's nothing wrong with using this technique, but to use it properly, your interest must be sincere, and you need to make an honest effort to understand. While Susan's technique for getting you to talk to her was good, her inattention caused it to backfire. Instead of liking her because she's interested in you, you end up resenting her because she's an insincere listener.

Poor timing, false agreement, outright dishonesty, or inattentiveness—whatever the cause of insincere listening, it's sure to destroy your effectiveness. To avoid being perceived as insincere, you only need conduct yourself in a way that conveys your sincerity toward the other person. First, *listen* carefully and *concentrate* on what the other person is saying. You'll always be attentive and will then automatically ask the *right* questions at the *right* time. Next, put yourself in the other person's shoes and imagine how he'll react to what *you* say. In this way you'll be sure not to be false or dishonest in your conversation because you know it will eventually catch up to you.

FIVE ACTION STEPS TO MAKE YOU A BETTER LISTENER

1. Remove the distractions that come into your mind through your thoughts, senses, and emotions so that you can concentrate on the speaker. Avoid playing the game of second-guessing and allow the speaker to complete his thoughts without adding your interruptions. Realize, though, that it is okay to ask for clarification if you aren't sure what his point is.

2. Maintain eye contact with the speaker and let your ears tune in as well. Block out other distractions so that the speaker has your total attention. Be animated and let your face reveal your inner feelings.

3. Aim for a balance of give-and-take rather than just asking a series of questions. Ask questions that require more than a short answer and offer information of your own. This gets the other

person to open up to you more readily and allows you to use your good listening skills.

4. Listen between the lines for the real message that is being communicated. Subtlety is a common human trait, and you will be valued as a good listener once you've learned to listen to more than just the words.

5. Avoid the traps of being labeled an insincere listener—poor timing in asking questions, false agreement or downright dishonesty, and inattentiveness. Put yourself in the speaker's place and imagine how he would react to what you say and how your behavior is reflecting your interest.

The guidelines that I've given you are both easy to follow and easy to build into your personality. Once they've become a habit, you'll be surprised how they'll increase your listening effectiveness and help you win and influence the people with whom you talk.

Chapter 7
HOW THE SUPER PERSUADER OPENS CLOSED MINDS

A man arrived home from work at the usual hour of five P.M. He discovered that it had not been one of his wife's better days. The result was a short fuse and an unpleasant attitude. Nothing he said or did was right. By seven P.M., things had not changed, so he suggested that he go outside, pretend that he had just gotten home, and start all over again. His wife agreed. He went outside, came back in, and announced, "Honey, I'm home!" "And just where have you been?" she replied sharply. "It's *seven o'clock!*"

One foggy night at sea, the captain of a ship saw what looked like the lights of another ship heading toward him. He had his signalman contact the other ship by light. The message was: "Change your course ten degrees to the south."

The reply came back: "Change *your* course ten degrees to the *north*."

Then the captain answered, "I am a captain, so change *your* course ten degrees to the *south*."

Reply: "I am a seaman first-class—change *your* course ten degrees to the *north*."

This last exchange really infuriated the captain, so he signaled back: "I am a battleship—change *your* course ten degrees to the *south*."

Reply: "And I am a lighthouse. Change *your* course ten degrees to the *north!*"

WHY DO PEOPLE RESIST CHANGE?

In this chapter we will discuss the nature of negativity, resistance to change, and basic techniques you can use to cope with difficult personalities. Have you ever wondered *why* people resist change, even when it's *beneficial* to them? A great deal of our resistance to change is based on a programmed need to be "right." One of the big fears we face in life is the fear of being "wrong." Being "right" means we're okay. We equate it with survival. Being "wrong" means we're *not* okay and is equated with the fear that we won't survive. So we're programmed to believe that the more "right" we are, the greater our chance of survival. This I'll refer to as the *Right-Wrong Syndrome*.

This can develop into a neurotic need to be right all the time. Most people would rather be right than be happy. In fact, we tend to reject *anyone* or *anything* that makes us wrong. More human failure can be attributed to our need to be right than any other source. How many times have you found it difficult to communicate because you were afraid of *saying* the "wrong" thing? Or you put off doing something because you were afraid you might do the wrong thing? Our self-image and self-esteem is tied into our need to be right.

SETTING UP PSYCHOLOGICAL POSITIONS

This encourages us to develop *psychological positions.* Psychological positions are highly conditioned verbal opinions that reside in our mind, often without our being aware of their existence. They are absolute prejudicial statements. Sometimes psychological positions may be simple racial or ethnic prejudices, but more often they are far more subtle and complex. They are highly organized propositions that *influence* what we *see,* what we *hear,* what we *think,* and what we *do.*

Not knowing about your positions or how to spot their existence in others reduces the probability of effective communication. Ignorance of these mechanisms makes constructive change almost impossible.

A major reason that psychological positions are difficult to dismiss is that people have a strong ingrained tendency to collect supporting evidence to prove that their position is "right." If a person believes that women are emotional rather than intellectual, any error in thinking made by a woman will be used as proof or evidence to support the position. If someone believes men are uncaring, any bit of insensitive male behavior will be collected as evidence to support that position.

Collecting evidence about people can affect your judgment. The difference between evidence and information is that information is not tainted by preconception. Information is scientifically or rationally gathered data that supports *what is,* not what we *feel or believe.*

There's another reason why people hold on to their positions. And that is that almost all positions have *partial* validity. For example, it is true that you sometimes make mistakes. No one is perfect. But making a mistake does not mean that you are an irresponsible, incompetent idiot. When you make a mistake, you may unknowingly activate someone's *perfectionist position.* In his mind you become an irresponsible, incompetent idiot because he believes mistakes equal imperfection, incompetence, and stupidity. No matter how unfair this conclusion may be, he will hold on to his opinion regardless of any argument to the contrary.

HOW PSYCHOLOGICAL POSITIONS MAKE IT DIFFICULT TO PERSUADE OTHERS

You have probably guessed that it is a waste of time to try to change the position of a person such as the perfectionist mentioned above. If you reply that you are not irresponsible or incompetent, he will remind you that you made a mistake. Since he cannot see the fallacy of his perfectionistic position, he will assume that you're just trying to avoid personal responsibility. And then he is likely to see you as being even more irresponsible, incompetent, and idiotic.

Positions influence people's perceptions, defenses, and actions. Here are some of the standard psychological positions we have observed in working with business people: people can't be trusted; change is dangerous; compromise is weak; one must be hardened to survive; it is dangerous to lose control; give an inch and they'll take a mile. All of these positions are aggressive in the sense of being hostile. People who ascribe to these statements tend to be authoritarian and unwilling to negotiate.

Positions that reflect a passive business orientation say things like this: showing feelings is weak; don't notice and it will go away; confrontation is dangerous; it's not my job; it doesn't matter; and the grass is always greener. These people are as closed to change as the authoritarian, and equally difficult to work with.

A person with a passive, or neutral, attitude perceives others as ineffectual. Others have little, if any, impact on the neutral person. Their inner message is: "Don't get involved." The neutral person lacks strong feelings toward others and rarely feels any emotional response when relating to other people. His position is: "People are unimportant and feelings don't count." His evidence is that no one allowed him to feel important when he was a child, and his feelings had no impact on the people around him. Since no one today can break through his wall of impassivity, he collects this as evidence that people have no impact.

The most difficult, and yet the most rewarding, thing that you can do is to become aware of your own psychological positions. Here are some hints to help you.

USING PSYCHOLOGICAL POSITIONS TO YOUR ADVANTAGE

Pay attention to your reactions in any interactional situation.

If you feel threatened in the absence of any real external danger, examine the cause of your anxiety; it could be a psychological position. For example, if you feel like you want to run away when the boss walks into your office, this may represent a position about yourself that says, "You're always doing something wrong" or "The boss is always out to get you."

Research has shown that your psychological positions are reinforced by thoughts or feelings that threaten you with dire consequences whenever you attempt to thwart those positions. If you challenge one of your positions, you may experience panic, fear, rage, depression, melancholy, or other negative feelings. For example, if you are friendly to strangers, contradicting an inner position you held that "strangers are dangerous," you may feel a deep sense of fear along with your friendliness.

To help you identify the positions of *others*, here are some things you can do.

Practice listening for the hidden meaning in a conversation. Notice any meaning that does not seem to fit the verbal context or the situation. For example, a jealous colleague may congratulate you on your raise, saying, "I knew you could get it if you tried hard enough" when he really means, "We all know you manipulated someone to get this raise. You don't really deserve it." His position is that it's a dog-eat-dog world. When you learn to recognize these hidden meanings, they often reflect a psychological position.

Look behind people's statements for possible positions. Analyze the content, word for word, and listen for innuendo and for incongruous usage of words. Listen for that flat tone of voice that implies a secret. Examine the body messages for incongruity. Does the person's posture conform to the meaning of the words? Does the tone of voice match the gestures?

Resistance reflects someone's positions. Resistance can reflect a bid for more time to think, a legitimate assessment process, or it can be a flat-out rejection of the premise before the argument is even heard. When you encounter resistance, try to ascertain whether it's caused by the fact that your statement threatens a position held by your opponent. Arguments that make little or no sense almost always indicate that a psychological position is at stake.

Strong value judgments may reflect a person's position. Someone may say, "My experience tells me that corporate executives are vicious." Is that based on corporate psychiatric testing, a resentful attitude toward successful people, or the influence of something the person has heard or read? Ask for the source of the person's value judgment. If the judgment is not based on rational data, it may express only a personal position.

Ask for definitions. A position is almost always indefensible and has a premise that is irrational or only partly valid. Asking for the definitions of each word might begin to clarify the issue.

When you are asked questions, be aware that the person may be looking for evidence to support one of his positions. It's not just the question per se but also tone of voice, facial expression, and general body message.

Concealing or restricting all nonverbal messages often expresses a psychological position. This is especially the case when a definite response is required by the situation. An extreme example of withholding is when a dissident member of a group is ostracized. The position here is: "You disobeyed the rules and deserve to be ignored. You do not exist."

When someone switches the topic of conversation abruptly, he is often defending a position. For example, a wife may say, "I think that we'd be better off in a new house. Let's sell this one." And the husband answers, "By the way, what ever happened to the garden hose?"

Like abrupt interruptions, disruptive behavior is usually a symptom of a personal position. The behavior may be talking loudly, throwing a temper tantrum, making noise, suddenly changing plans, or acting irrationally.

The psychological position is usually based on scanty or prejudicial data. Therefore, uncovering the position and exposing it to the light of day defeats its purpose and makes it useless. Here are some various methods for handling the positions of others.

Ignoring the position cancels its power. This can be effective, since the efficacy of a position is founded on power manipulation. Be aware, though, that ignoring the position may escalate the attempt to collect evidence to support the position. This happens because the position-holder feels that the position is necessary for survival. When other people ignore the position, the validity of the position is challenged and there is a frantic effort to gather more evidence.

You can confront the individual by asking what data supports his position. Confrontation brings the situation to the surface for examination. Most positions don't hold up under close scrutiny.

When subjected to an attack from a psychological position, one can deflect its effect. For example, a manager says, "You are just like all the rest of those women." A good communicator might answer, "You must be frustrated with women. I'm sorry your experience has been so negative."

When addressing an adversary, you can ask them to tell you the consequences they anticipate if they were to give up this position. Ask: "What are your fears, and what can I do about them?"; "What does your anger mean, and what can I do about your anger?"; "How will you be rejected, and how can I prevent that from happening?"

FEAR IS THE MAJOR CAUSE OF A CLOSED MIND

The advocates of winning through the use of intimidation rarely mention the role of fear or anger; fear is, however, a major cause of most conflict. Fear is what a person feels when confronted by a real or an assumed danger. It is a highly complex emotion and often leads to attacks and consequences that people do not understand.

People typically react to danger and the fear it produces by fighting, or fleeing, in order to survive. A fight-or-flight reaction might have been essential to survival in prehistoric or primitive stages of human development, but today, such a response, will, unfortunately, cause more problems than it will solve. A frightened person may flee from the benefits you want to share with him. Or he may attack your judgment out of the fear that you are being deceptive. You must be ready to address and dispel this fear. Obviously you cannot react to the stress this attack produces on you as primitive man might have, by screaming and running out, or giving the person a thump on the head.

Fear, of either a physical or a psychological nature, will be the major reason why people refuse to cooperate with you, even when it is in their best interests to do so. They may fear losing the rewards you promise, or they may fear financial loss or looking like a fool to themselves or others.

Much resistance can be reduced by dealing openly with the concepts that frighten the individual. There's no better way than to: (1) accept and support his right to feel fear; (2) formulate and confirm a question about it; and (3) answer the question to his satisfaction. Let's look more closely at each step.

HELPING OTHERS TO REDUCE THEIR FEAR

Accept a person's emotions by admitting that his feelings are reasonable and not unusual under the circumstances. By doing this you will cause him to think more clearly about the reward you are offering him, and you will show that you understand his conflicts. It will also help steer away from an either/or choice for which he is not ready. If you refuse to accept a person's fears as important, he will think that you question his intelligence or emotional stability. And you will have destroyed any rapport that you may have established.

The next step is to turn the resistance into a request for additional information. Most of the time an objection is actually such a request, though you have to make the other person aware of it. While accepting his feelings, help him realize that he needs more information by saying, "I think I understand your question better now," and then rephrase his objection as a question. Naturally you should answer the question you have brought into focus for him. (It's also important that you are perceptive to his nonverbal signs as well as what he has to say.) Even if he rejects your attempt to focus his interest by stating that you have missed the mark, you will not have reduced his trust if your attempts have not been threatening or dismissive. You can openly ask what is really bothering him and thus give him permission to be honest with you.

To reassure another about the reward you have to offer, a short story about someone who benefited in a similar manner can be used. Use the words *feel, felt,* and *found.* "Quite a few people *feel* the way you do. Joe Smith *felt* much the same way. But after he decided to try, he *found* . . ."

Another good way to avoid conflict is through a compromising technique called the law of reciprocity. This lets you come away with the half a loaf, and that is your key to consistent winning. It enables *both* people to remain in their comfort zones and to avoid the stress that leads to immature behavior. The technique is based on the fact that all of our feelings are legitimate and necessary for survival. Thus, when no *great issues*, or *struggles for survival*, are at stake, you can gain acceptance and support by compromising through reciprocity rather than raising resistance and resentment with the law of the jungle.

HOW TO DEAL WITH AN ANGRY PERSON

The more demanding or intense a relationship, the more likely the chance that conflicts will arise. Actually, any good manager wants his subordinates competing for his job when he's promoted. A teacher wants students to strive for knowledge and skill. Parents want their children to mature to self-control and achievement. These are examples, however, of appropriate competition; few raw conflicts are productive. Most of them cause an emotional distress that *lowers* commitment and dedication. But many conflicts can be solved *before* the participants have been forced *too far* from their comfort zone, if the following control technique is used.

The steps of the conflict control technique are:

1. *Accept* the speaker's complaints without rejection. Be an active listener who really hears what the words convey.

2. *Share* the speaker's concern by agreeing or em-

pathizing. Say, "I see what you mean" or "I'd feel the same way if I were in your shoes."

3. *Reflect* the speaker's feelings to demonstrate understanding. You can paraphrase his statements after saying something like, "Let's see if I understand what you are saying."

4. *Advocate new* information to help him change his mind. He needs a logical reason to agree with you, so offer one that will keep him from seeming *indecisive*.

5. *Confirm* his agreement by asking for *acceptance*. Get him to commit himself verbally, to close the issue on a positive note.

Acceptance, sharing, and *reflection* are the most effective tools when dealing with an angry person's emotions. These first three steps allow him to gain relief, to return to his comfort zone. Once this happens he can more effectively deal with the facts in the final two steps—*advocating* and *confirmation*. The method most people use reverses the order and deals with the facts first and emotions later, if at all. By using the five-step method, understanding and acceptance can be maintained, even when it is not possible to find a compromise or grant partial fulfillment.

When solutions are *not* negotiable and you have to require cooperation or compliance, it can still be done in a way to assure that good relations continue. As in many cases, it's not *what* you do but *how* you do it. This is so because most people prefer a mutually supportive relationship to winning all the time. Offering support when an occasional payoff must be withheld can be accomplished effectively by using the supportive refusal technique. Here are the steps to using the *supportive refusal technique*.

First of all, accept the person's request in supportive terms. Acceptance, as it always does, lets another person gain emotional relief without receiving rebuttal, which would devalue him. Next, express understanding by paraphrasing the request.

Put his feelings into your own words to show that you really know how he feels. Then, state the legitimate denial in authentic terms. This gives him something to reason about once you have accepted and supported his emotions. Next, help the person be authentic about his feelings. Helping the disappointed person express his feelings clears the air and offers more symbolic relief. Finally, restate the denial firmly but supportively. Restating the denial in a firm but noncritical manner helps gain acceptance and close the issue permanently.

The supportive refusal forms a clear, logical answer to a disappointed or angry person with whom you cannot negotiate the outcome, except to give him acceptance and support. It takes a little more time than a blunt no, but it shows your genuine concern for the person's feelings. It also avoids the weaknesses of a long, unstructured discussion because it addresses the critical emotional issues.

Most of the refusals that complicate your attempts to include people in mutual payoffs occur because people are afraid of getting hurt. Fear not only makes people *flee* from you, it also makes them *fight*. Even situations seemingly stemming from blatant selfishness are usually the result of someone's fear—fear of not getting what he deserves for his time, money, or self—or from his need to be right.

FIVE ACTION STEPS TO HELP OPEN CLOSED MINDS

1. Never fight back in response to a criticism. Rather, you can compliment the critic if he has made an important observation. Often just a little praise and recognition disarms critics and changes their attitude toward you. Remember that they are responding this way because in some way you have hit the "hot button" of a psychological position they hold.

2. Neutralize objections by restating them as a question and a request for more information. Then answer the question or draw out the *real* objection.

3. On a piece of paper list the advantages of your idea or proposal on one side and the disadvantages on the other. If the points that you have presented have merit, the choice is self-evident.

4. Timing is of the essence. Address emotional needs with support and understanding first, or your logical facts will never be heard.

5. Your message will never be communicated if you attempt to make the other person look wrong in order to make you look right. Explain that you are both trying to come up with the best solution for the situation, and allow him to change his mind gracefully and almost unnoticeably.

Following these suggestions doesn't mean that you will handle *every* difficult opponent. But it will, more importantly, make *you* feel better about the way you handle *yourself*. You will find, as you do these things, that persuading others will become a peaceful, and largely conflict-free, experience.

Chapter 8
HOW SUPER PERSUADERS GIVE AND RECEIVE CRITICISM EFFECTIVELY

There is a sign in some kitchens that reads, COMPLAINTS TO THE COOK CAN BE HAZARDOUS TO YOUR HEALTH! This is a reflection of our attitude toward criticism. Most of us welcome honest feedback—as long as it is flattering and complimentary. People in leadership roles of any kind, whether in the home, classroom, or office, realize that there are times when they have to demand better performance, punish someone who has refused to cooperate, or set some issue straight. Regardless of your good intentions at such a time, correction and criticism is not pleasant to the person receiving your attention. You can, however, improve your skills at correcting people so that it does not cost you goodwill and cooperation.

WHY SHOULD WE TAKE CRITICISM?

The definition of criticism is *pointing out a fault*. This is also known as negative feedback. That raises the question of why have negative feedback at all. We prefer to get compliments and praise because it makes us feel good. So why have criticism at all?

I'm sure as a child you played a game where somebody hid something in the room, then you had the person leave the room, and when they came back in, you would give them a message of hot or cold as the person got closer or farther away from that object. So we need balance: hot and cold; positive and negative. Criticism is an effective learning experience. Successful people in this world are not people who *avoid* mistakes or errors. They're the ones who *learn* from them. And we all make mistakes. Henry Ford, in inventing the automobile, made one big mistake the first time around—he left out reverse.

THREE REACTIONS TO CRITICISM

We all have some problems in responding to criticism. Criticism tends to stir up any number of strong emotional feelings, from guilt and resentment to outright anger. There are three ways of handling criticism. Notice which one you fall into when *taking* criticism. The first reaction is *fight*. In saying, "I don't want to hear about it," you *deny* the criticism; you turn it down and fight it. If someone criticizes you, your response may be, "You're out of your mind" or "Keep your opinions to yourself." In this case you are fighting the criticism.

The second way of handling criticism is *flight*. When you're using flight, you're saying, "Don't criticize me, because I can't face it; I can't discuss it," and you might think, "How can I be so stupid?" or "I never do anything right." You might start crying or become overwhelmed by it. Now flight might seem to be the opposite of fight—fight is aggressive and flight is timid—but actually they have more in common than you might realize. In both reactions you *deny* the criticism. In saying, "I don't want to talk about it," whether it be through tears or aggression, you are denying the issue. These two reactions are both refusals to examine the truth.

The third reaction is to *evaluate*. This is where we've been advised by our parent figures to be objective and open-minded. The problem is that evaluation is easier said than done. When you tell me to be objective, how do I go about doing that? Here are some steps to evaluate criticism.

1. Ask yourself, "What can I learn from this person?" There's something to be learned if you look for it.

2. Agree with *part* of the criticism. If you do that, here's what you will accomplish. You will let the person know that he has been heard. You get out of the whole argument that says, "You haven't been listening to me." You've indicated, "Yes, I have mentally processed that comment." You're admitting, "I'm not perfect and I can stand some improvement." When you do this, you take the wind out of their sails. If you say, "You know there's some truth in what you're telling me about that," then you don't have an opponent.

3. Be sure you *understand* the criticism. Many times we get criticized, and it's not really clear what the person is getting at. This is because it is stated in generalized terms instead of behavioral terms. It's a fact that criticism is often phrased in a way that's not very useful. If you don't understand the criticism, question the person in a calm, information-seeking tone of

voice, not a threatening one. Question that person to find out exactly what they mean. Now, that's hard to do if you have a fight reaction, so remind yourself that you must ask one question. Say to them, "Tell me more about your viewpoint."

4. Take time out and say, "I'd like to think about that and then I'll call you back tomorrow morning." Give yourself time to digest the criticism before responding.

5. Analyze and get the facts. Good data makes good decisions.

6. Adjust your behavior if *you* decide to. Many people feel that they're being forced to change when they're criticized, and no wonder they fight back. But it's your decision. Keep in mind what you can learn from the criticism.

We're talking about *taking* criticism first because we've been advised to be empathetic with others so that we understand what they're going through. If we know how to *take* criticism, we also have a sensitivity because we've been examining how *we* feel. When a criticism is stated, it is given from that person's viewpoint, and it's one person's way of looking at a situation. So when you give criticism, you are saying, "This is *my* viewpoint." When giving criticism, here are some opening lines to avoid:

This is none of my business, but . . .
Don't get angry but . . .

In using these phrases you are implanting the idea that you're going to do the very thing you're claiming to avoid. This is an attempt to be tactful and is not successful. The negative suggestion will stay in the person's mind rather than the disclaimer.

WHY SHOULD WE GIVE CRITICISM?

When is it appropriate to give criticism? Is honesty enough of a reason? Many hurtful statements are made in the name of honesty. There's a saying that I like that goes, "There's honesty and there is brutality; but there's no such thing as brutal honesty." In fact, you can be sure that if anyone comes up to you and says, "Let me be perfectly honest . . ." it's not going to be a compliment! In fact, it's going to be a real zinger, and the pretext of "honesty" is only an attempt to sugarcoat the attack. Honesty alone is not a good enough reason to give criticism. Here are some reasons to give criticism:

1. *Responsibility.* If you're a supervisor and you answer for the work of your subordinates, it's important for you to use criticism because you have to set job standards. This is shown very clearly when a secretary types a letter for you. If there are errors in the letter, you're signing your name to that person's work, and so you're accountable and need to give criticism to guide that person's performance.

2. *Parenting.* As a parent you're responsible for some of your child's behavior, and so it's important to criticize them to correct that behavior.

3. *Protecting human rights.* Supposing you're riding in a car with someone and they're speeding along. You have a right to say to that person, "Don't drive so fast" because you have a right to stay alive. And so you need to give the criticism. You might say, "I'm uncomfortable with you driving at that speed and I'd like you to slow down." You have a right to give this type of criticism.

4. *Intimate relationships.* We tell intimate friends or mates things we wouldn't tell others. We

might discuss their haircut or their skirt length or their clothes, and we're doing this to be supportive to these people. Realize that this is not a license to kill. We still need to have tact and sensitivity.

5. *Crisis*. In a crisis situation you simply yell out the criticism and make it a command and it's instantly given. There's no time to say, "Well, let's talk about this." The crisis calls for criticism on the spot. If you want people to accept your criticism, you have to build a trust level, and this trust level comes *before* the criticism. That means that at other times you're praising those people to whom the criticism is addressed.

Set standards in advance. Let people know what you require. You'll have much less resentment from a person when you give criticism, if they know the standards in advance. Also provide privacy. If you're going to give criticism, take the person aside or shut the door. Remove any audience attention and avoid an impersonal situation. Let them know that you're not playing to an audience. This will keep their emotions in perspective and help them concentrate on the *issue*.

Also, seek information before you begin criticizing someone. Suppose you see someone just standing around on the job and you go tell that person what you think of that kind of behavior. Before you do that, you might say to yourself, "Seek information first," and go over to them and say, "You know, I've noticed you standing here for about thirty minutes. Tell me more about that. What's the reason?" And then that person might tell you that they're on a special assignment, that the president of the company asked them to stand there and wait for the package that was going to be delivered. If you'd

given him that criticism for just standing
around, you would have been embarrassed.

Be constructive, be specific and use behavioral terms in
your criticism. Give the criticism of the behavior, not the person. For example, if the person is using poor English, perhaps
a double negative, you wouldn't want to go up to them and
say, "Your English is terrible," because then you're criticizing
the person and not their behavior. And the person doesn't
know what to change. It might be better to say, "You know
you're using a double negative, and if you say it this way,
that's the correct way." It's irritating to people when you are
not specific. So it's important, then, to criticize the performance, not the performer. Use words that deal with future
improvement. A poor choice would be "Don't mess this up
like you did last time" because this is a negative affirmation
that you put on that person. Look to the future, speak in terms
of improvement, and say to them, "The next time I'd like you
to do it this way."

Deal in things, not personalities. If you criticize the person
instead of their behavior, they will consider it a personal attack. If you say to them, "You are a sloppy typist," then that
person will become resentful and angry and will sabotage you
the next time they type something. A better choice would be,
"This letter has five mistakes, and it needs to be typed again."
Again, deal with things rather than attacking the person with
labels or personal descriptions.

A BETTER WAY TO USE THE
SANDWICH TECHNIQUE

In communication, there is something that is known as the
sandwich or the *oreo-cookie technique*. It has three parts: the
cookie, the filling, and the other cookie. The first cookie is

positive comment. You tell the other person that you like and appreciate them and what they are doing. Then, in between, you put in the negative—what you don't like or what you want them to improve. Then you end on a positive note, expressing a belief that things will get better. By expressing trust in the person's ability to improve, you have given the person permission to change without losing face. So you have the positive, the negative, and the positive. I'm sure you can see that the theory is that you leave the person with a pleasant thought.

Unfortunately this technique is sometimes used so indiscriminately that when you receive a compliment, you start to think, "Here comes the negative." You start to get paranoid when somebody compliments you. If you have a problem with the sandwich technique, I would like to give you an additional formula called EFA. It is an *empathetic* remark, a *factual* remark, and a *call for action*. For example, you are in a restaurant that is very busy and you have a problem getting service. You recognize that the waitress is busy, and if you don't give criticism just the right way, she's probably going to break down in tears, or worse, she'll probably try to get revenge on you and punish you. Now you may have either a fight or a flight reaction. Using the EFA principle, you would say to the waitress, "I realize you're very busy." This is empathetic. You're saying to the waitress, "I understand where you're coming from." Number two is factual. You say, "I have an appointment." Don't apologize for the appointment or qualify it or say, "I know this isn't your fault, but . . ." Just state a plain fact: "I have an appointment in thirty minutes." Then number three, a call for action, again without apology, say, "I need to have my food served immediately." Be assertive, considerate, and clear and direct.

HOW THE SUPER PERSUADER CAN USE CONSTRUCTIVE CONFRONTATION

It's emotionally painful to discover that your efforts do not meet the expectations of others. Criticism causes us to get our feelings hurt and our sensitivities stepped on. By the same token, you may dread *giving* criticism because you vividly recall your own discomfort at *taking* criticism. And you may put off a confrontation and let simple problems grow out of proportion.

Constructive confrontation may be described as a deliberate attempt to help another person examine the consequences of some aspect of his behavior. It is an invitation to self-examination. Confrontation is a way of expressing concern for another person and a wish to increase the mutual involvement in the relationship. The purpose of a confrontation is to free the person being confronted so they can engage in more fruitful or less destructive behavior. Here are some guidelines.

1. Do not confront another person if you do not intend to increase your involvement with him. You need to consider what to say, why it is important to say it, what the real motives are for saying it, how the person will react, how you can help them deal nondefensively with the data —to understand and internalize it—to become aware of the implications, and what the alternatives for future choices are. To do less is not an act stemming from the desire to help, but is probably hostility.

2. Confront only if you experience feelings of caring. The only honest reason for offering a confrontation is the belief that awareness of the information will enhance the present and future well-being of the person.

3. Confront only if the relationship has gone beyond the initial stages of development or if basic trust has been established.

4. Make sure a person's defensiveness is under control. Otherwise, he will discount the information and alienation is a likely outcome.

Some statements seem to faciliate in-depth interaction, self-examination, and beliefs, while others seem to block that process. Here are some blocks to open communication:

- *Put-downs and personal criticisms*—"You've got to be kidding when you say that!"

- *Rejection of feelings*—"Come on, there's no reason for you to be upset."

- *Giving advice or pressing for a course of action before the relevant facts are known*—"Why don't you just go tell your boss off."

- *Giving an opinion, especially if it is offered so that there is no room to present another point of view.*

- *Asking a series of interrogating, data-gathering questions, or why questions that require justification*—"Why did you do a dumb thing like that?"

- *Giving support in a patronizing way*—"Lots of people feel that way"—or *lecturing, moralizing, and sermonizing*—"When I was a child . . ."

To open and broaden communication channels and stimulate a more in-depth level of thinking, you may choose one of these responses:

1. Summarize what you have heard.

2. Respond to the other person's feelings and beliefs without judging them.

3. Request clarification. You might say, "I'm not sure I understand. Can you give me another example of when this has happened?"

4. Give *I* messages, such as, "I'm eager to know what you did" or "I'm disappointed that things didn't work out as you had hoped."

5. Make low-level inferences. For example, you may say, "I sense that you were very disappointed" or "I have a hunch that it was very difficult for you to do that."

These responses allow people to broaden their relationships to include differing interests, points of view, and experiences.

THE CORRECT METHOD OF USING COMPLIMENTS

There are also, of course, situations in which compliments are appropriate. A realistic statement of a person's capacities, capabilities, resources, and good qualities at a time when he or she is discouraged or faced with a difficult situation is very helpful and constructive. At such a time it is particularly important to be precise, clear, and concrete, since people often find it hard to believe compliments when they are feeling low, and it is important to give proof, or substance, to these compliments by using facts and logic. When evaluating someone, the positive statements should be as numerous, clear, and detailed as the criticisms.

The highest compliment is one that shows the perception of a talent, a strength, or a belief in the person before he or she is aware of it. Such a compliment makes the person aware of this hidden portion of the self in such a way that that quality is brought to blossom. This form of compliment is appropriate at any time.

Compliments are helpful in disagreements and discussions. If they are honest and apt, they ease the tension of confrontation and make a productive outcome more likely. Compliments that show respect and appreciation for the honesty and goodwill of one's opponent make it possible for the opponent to look at the possibility of being wrong without feeling badly about himself. For instance, a poor response in a disagreement would be, "You are all wrong because your premise is wrong." A good response would be, "Your position is clearly and logically stated. Unfortunately I can't agree with your premise because..." Because respect was shown to the speaker's skill in the second example, he is more likely not to hold on to his position out of pride, and he is less likely to develop personal animosity.

Compliments should be true and honest. For example, to tell someone, "I'm sure you'll succeed because you have so much enthusiasm," is not true. You can't be sure that another person will succeed. Such a statement may be harmful by keeping that person from doing important self-examination. Saying, "You've got a lot of enthusiasm, which should be a great help in undertaking what you want to do," is an accurate and encouraging statement and doesn't set up unrealistic expectations.

Compliments should be freeing, not restricting. Talk about the person and what he does, not about products, conclusions, or things. To say, "You have good color awareness in clothes," is better than saying, "That is a pretty dress." The first statement encourages the person to choose more freely; the second statement ties her to her present style of dress. Likewise, to say, "That is a great idea," ties one to the idea, while the statement, "You really think things through," encourages one to think more deeply about things.

And so we've learned that productive criticism or correction, which leads to winning relationships, deals with only the important issues and how to correct mistakes. Character flaws and problems of motivation and commitment must be considered only when the atmosphere is calm and when authentic praise can be used to counteract the unpleasantness the criticism is sure to produce. Even at that time, however, you can use terms and concepts that are supportive and lead to higher expectations for the future.

In dealing with your anger and the anger of others, remember that people are rarely consistent emotionally. We all have peaks and valleys as our feelings ebb and flow. It is inevitable that at some time or another, others will become frustrated and in turn will frustrate you despite your best efforts to keep things going smoothly. Remember that few people have the insights into human attitudes and behavior that you do as a result of reading this book. Using the information and methods given here can prepare you for times of frustration and help you nip problem situations in the bud with acceptance and support from those you are criticizing and confronting.

FIVE ACTION STEPS TO HELP YOU GIVE AND TAKE CRITICISM EFFECTIVELY

1. Present the data on which your inferences are based before stating the inference. Have actual information available and avoid words such as *always* and *never*.

2. Complain directly to the person involved and not to anyone else. Don't compare their behavior to that of other people; and make your complaint, in private, as soon as you can, since waiting allows anger to build.

3. Criticize only those things that the person has the capacity to change, noting the faults in the

performance and not the performer. There is no need for you to apologize for your complaint, to use sarcasm, or to ask for their motivation in doing that to which you object. Prefacing your criticism with, "This is for your own good," will in all likelihood destroy the chances that your remarks will be accepted in a friendly spirit.

4. Use the Oreo-cookie technique (positive comment, negative comment showing the area for improvement, positive comment expressing the hope for better performance in the future) or the EFA technique (empathetic remark, a factual remark, and a call for action). If you never compliment the other person, don't expect him always to remain open to your criticism. It is also a good practice to thank people for *listening* to your criticism.

5. In accepting criticism, listen to what the critic has to say without speaking or discouraging him, rephrase the criticism in your mind in terms of ways you choose to act, use your intelligence to help *articulate* the objections rather than *obscure* them, and ask the critic politely what suggestions he may have as alternatives. Thank anyone who offers honest criticism— especially those who have nothing to gain and possibly something to lose. Once you discover that criticism doesn't have to destroy your confidence, friendships, or career, you can go a long way in improving all three.

Chapter 9
USING HUMOR TO INCREASE YOUR POWER OF SUPER PERSUASION

Have you ever wondered what *causes* a smile, a laugh, or rollicking laughter? Philosophers, comedians, and psychologists have asked this question for many years. *There's no answer,* and that is part of the fun. Aristotle thought that an ugliness or defect, which is not painful or destructive, is comic. Kant believed it was the sudden transformation of a strained expectation into nothing; failing to get what you want; or, even funnier, getting what you don't want. Charlie Chaplin defined humor as "playful pain." People laugh when they see someone fall down, but if that person doesn't get up, they'll stop laughing. Chaplin was the little tramp who took the kicks of the world and walked out of every picture, away from defeat that he had somehow turned to triumph.

WHAT IS HUMOR?

There are many definitions of humor. It seems best described as "nervous susceptibility to incongruence." A person laughs when there is a contrast between what a thing or situation is perceived to be and what it's supposed to be. If a person falls into the water with his bathing suit on, we don't laugh. But if he falls in wearing his street clothes, that's incongruous and will strike most people as funny.

An executive-search firm found that executives under thirty-five had a lesser sense of humor than their older counterparts. People have become more serious and cynical, perhaps because of international and economic tensions. This attitude is reflected in how we see our lives and our various roles.

The same study revealed, too, that as executives got older and more mature in their attitudes, they gained confidence, perspective, *and* humor. The researchers concluded that young executives who show no humor on the job are missing an important lesson. Success in any profession depends on influencing others. And a sparkling wit is still the best way to do it.

USING HUMOR IN A CRISIS SITUATION

All businesses, from the most complex corporate structure to the mom-and-pop store, place a high value on humor. Top executives rely on their sense of humor to control their image and how the public views their companies. This is especially true in a crisis when a company's image is at stake. Here the executive can make or break the company with the way he handles the crisis. When Chrysler chairman, Lee Iacocca, was faced with the company's financial trouble, he volunteered to reduce his salary to one dollar a year. One of his shareholders asked him to comment on this, and Iacocca replied, "Don't worry, I'll spend it very carefully."

Iacocca was able to find humor in his situation because he

could consider the question from a different point of view. By finding a new perspective on a troubled, embarrassing, or discouraging situation, *you* can redirect *your* thinking to new ways of dealing with the problem. This removes you from the immediate situation and allows you to get a bigger picture. From this vantage point crises don't seem so terrible or permanent. Keeping a jovial outlook gives you a sense of security in the middle of chaos. A well-aimed humorous remark is a lot better than giving up in defeat or trying to escape the situation.

A change of perspective can also make you more effective with the people with whom you work. Mentally detach yourself from the situation and the people with whom you are working. Stand back, as if you were watching a play. At once, the roles of the people you observe come into focus and appear in a completely different light.

Taking risks is an important part of our lives. The ability to know *when* to take a risk is very important. Keeping a sense of humor when considering risks can be *useful*. When you try to do something risky and it fails, your sense of humor can save you from further insult or damage. Demonstrating humor in tense situations is risky in itself, but you can use it to your advantage to show your associates that you are human and sometimes make mistakes. When we take the initiative in admitting mistakes, people tend to be less critical. Revealing our own faults and mistakes leads to our own self-knowledge, which leads to self-confidence and improved performance. An active sense of humor is a trait many companies look for in their executives. It's an indication that the person has an active, flexible mind, that he doesn't take himself too seriously, and that even if he errs once in a while, he is capable of making better decisions in the future.

THE PHYSICAL EFFECTS OF HUMOR

We've seen that when people are in a tense business and social situation, humor will relieve psychological stress, but it has a positive *physical* effect for us too.

In 1976, publisher Norman Cousins wrote about laughing himself to recovery from a degenerative spinal condition. Doctors had told him that his illness may have been caused by adrenal (kidney) exhaustion. The endocrine imbalance (meaning the balance of hormonal secretions in the bloodstream) can be caused by negative emotions, such as tension, frustration, or suppressed rage. Cousins had read about the endocrine system's role in fighting disease. He wondered: If negative emotions can harm you physically, can positive emotions help you?

Doctors gave Cousins a 1 in 500 chance of survival, but rather than accept their decision, he took matters into his own hands. He checked out of the hospital and into a hotel room. He ordered several tapes of the *Candid Camera* television shows and other humorous films and books. With these, Cousins gave himself a treatment program of belly laughter that worked as an anesthesia for relieving some of his pain. Within a few years he had recovered fully, and now he lectures all over the world about his "laugh therapy."

While some doctors said that Cousins would have recovered, anyway, others seriously began to study the biology of laughter. Some new discoveries in the chemical research and the mental health fields have given the old saying, "Laughter is the best medicine," a brand-new meaning.

Laughter is just plain good exercise. It gives the diaphragm, thorax, abdomen, heart, and lungs a good workout. Muscles in the abdomen, chest, shoulders, and elsewhere contract; the heart rate and blood pressure increase; the pulse can double from 60 to 120. A good belly laugh has the *same effect* as running in place!

Laughter also can relieve some state-of-the-mind discomforts: boredom, tension, guilt, depression, headaches and backaches. It stimulates the brain to produce certain hormones that trigger the release of *endorphins,* proteins produced naturally within the brain that reduce pain or discomfort, release tension, and give us extra energy.

There's a good deal of evidence to show that the person with a healthy sense of humor has better healing qualities and better effectiveness on the job.

Psychologists regard the humor-making aspect of human beings as a means of actualizing the self and coping with life's ups and downs. Humor helps you from getting stuck in annoying situations. Through it you become more than the person who can't find a parking place, or the one who just blew the Jones account. You can say to yourself, "This situation is absurd, *but I'm not.*"

FOUR TYPES OF HUMOR

There are many kinds of humor. You have probably noticed all of them in your surroundings.

First, there is *hostile humor*. This is making people laugh by hurting someone else. In an office, for example, the boss might say in front of everyone in the room, "Miss Jones, you have been here two weeks, and already you are one month behind in your work."

The second kind is *superiority humor*. This is laughing at someone else's inferiority. On his first visit to New York, a small-town visitor managed to stop at all the bars in Times Square before he stumbled down a stairway leading to the subway. Emerging half an hour later, he met a friend who had been looking for him. "Where have you been?" the friend asked. "Down in some guy's cellar," the man replied, glassy-eyed, "and, boy, has he got a set of trains!"

The third type of humor is *authority-rebellion humor*. The following anecdote from the writings of Winston Churchill is a good example of this approach. On one occasion Churchill submitted a written speech that was to be distributed to the London press. A young Oxford civil servant read the speech and sent it back to Churchill with the following message written in the margin, "My dear Prime Minister, I hardly think it is fitting for the Prime Minister of England to dangle his participles or end his sentences in prepositions. Kindly correct before distribution." Churchill read this and sent it back with the following note in the other margin, "My dear young man, This is the sort of criticism up with which I will not put!"

The fourth type is *philosophical humor*. This is perhaps the highest form of humor. It is the humor of mature people expressing honest curiosity. It is poking fun at human beings when they are foolish or forget their place in the universe. Lincoln's humor is a good example. Lincoln probably never made a joke that hurt anybody else. Indeed, many of his jokes had an educational function beyond the laugh. One day when Lincoln was walking along a Springfield road, he approached a man who was driving by in a carriage. Lincoln asked the man if he would take his overcoat to town. "With pleasure," the man said, "but how will you get it back again?"

"Very readily," said Lincoln, "I intend to remain in it."

USING HUMOR TO YOUR ADVANTAGE

To harness the power of humor in your communications, here are some easy techniques that you can use. If it is a *formal* setting, comment on the flattering introduction. At a convention of the American Bar Association, the chairman introduced Adlai Stevenson. When Stevenson stood up to give his speech, he said, "I was a little worried as Mr. Craig was giving that wonderful introduction. I began to think that he was going to introduce Benjamin Franklin."

You can also belittle your position in order to gain more respect from the listeners' initiative. Oliver Wendell Holmes once said, "I am a professor emeritus, which means pretty nearly the same thing as a tired-out or a worn-out instructor."

You can poke fun at yourself. Joan Rivers says, "I was a homely kid. When the other boys in the neighborhood played doctor, I was the receptionist."

You can describe a funny happening. General Douglas MacArthur used this technique in his farewell speech to West Point cadets. MacArthur had graduated at the top of his class at West Point and later became its superintendent. He said, "As I was leaving the hotel this morning a doorman asked me where I was bound. And when I replied, 'West Point,' he remarked, 'Beautiful place. Have you ever been there before?'" With those few remarks, MacArthur, austere in appearance and solemn in the manner of a five-star general, showed that he wasn't a stuffed shirt.

You can tell an amusing anecdote about yourself. Author Mortimer J. Adler tells the story of stopping in a jewelry store to pick up a gift. The jeweler, who had a passing acquaintance with his customer, posed a question. "What do you do, Mr. Adler?" he asked. "I'm a philosopher," replied Adler. The jeweler looked dismayed. "No," he said, "I meant what do you do for a *living?*"

You can use humor to identify with your listener. Mark Twain once said to the New England Society, "I reverently believe that the Maker who made us all, makes everything in New England—but the weather."

New York Bishop Fulton Sheen was especially noted for his wit. He once said that he thought applause summed up the highest Christian virtues. He felt that if anyone clapped before he spoke, they were expressing *faith*. If anyone clapped in the middle of his talk, he thought they were expressing *hope*. And if anyone clapped at the end, it was an act of *charity*.

There are various functions of humor. You can use it effectively to dramatize a point. Two astronauts scheduled for a lunar mission were simulating some procedures on a Navajo Indian reservation in Arizona. The terrain there was similar to the moon's surface, and the duo needed practice.

A Navajo medicine man spotted the space-suited pair and asked the chief who the funny-looking guys were. Told they were going to the moon, the medicine man said that according to legend, some Navajos had once gone to the moon. Perhaps the spacemen would deliver a message to them for him.

The astronauts readily agreed. Since the Navajo language is not a written one, a tape recorder was used. Curious, the astronauts asked the medicine man what the nature of his message was. Translated, it meant, "Beware of these two. They'll try to make a treaty with you."

You can use humor to lay the groundwork for a serious point. A college professor, to make his point, told his class that W. C. Fields was once asked, "How do you like children?" His answer was, "Well cooked." The professor went on to say that "no one, no matter how humane, can stand to be in the presence of an adolescent twenty-four hours a day, but if you're going to be a teacher," he said, "it helps if you like kids."

Humor can advance your central theme. The distinguished lawyer and politician William Jennings Bryan told the following story:

Some years ago a celebrity returned to his alma mater, a small college in the West. After a speech in the chapel by the visitor, the president of the college asked him if he would like to visit the room that he had while he was a student there. The celebrity said that he would be delighted to, and so the two men crossed the campus to the old dormitory and knocked at the door.

Now it happened that the present occupant of the room was digging out his Latin with the help of a fair coed—a violation of the rule forbidding girls to visit the boys' dorm. The boy suspected that his caller may be a faculty member, and so he told the girl to hide in the closet. She did, and he answered the door.

The president presented his distinguished guest and explained why they were there. The celebrity looked around the room and smiled. "Ah, the same old table and the same old chairs." He went to the window. "Yes, even the same old tree." He turned back and said, "The same old closet," and opened the door. He saw the coed and exclaimed, "And the same old girl."

The student spoke up. "My sister, sir."

"And the same old lie," replied the celebrity.

From here, Bryan moved on to the same old lies that his political opponents were telling.

Humor can give your ideas vivid illustration. In getting people to rally their forces behind you, you can use the story about the young man who approached a father about marrying his daughter. The father was skeptical and said, "I doubt very much that you would be able to support my daughter. I can hardly do it myself." The young man then offered the bright suggestion, "We'll just have to pool our resources!"

As a memory device, you can't beat the power of a story. It's amazing how often we forget what someone has said, but the stories they told stay with us. Humorous stories can be powerful vehicles for driving home your message. They appeal to the emotions and get people involved. Most stories are personal experiences, so you aren't just *telling*—you're *relating*, which means you're *feeling*. Stories are a friendly gesture. They gain attention. They have universal appeal. They take the known—what you can hear, see, and feel—to the unknown and the abstract.

DEVELOPING YOUR OWN SPECIAL SENSE OF HUMOR

Now here are some specific techniques that you can use to develop your own sense of humor.

Develop a sense of irreverence. Few of us are so naïve and unsophisticated as not to be aware that we are amply supplied with the vanity, stupidity, greed, dishonesty, and hypocrisy to deny the same! Become aware that there's a funny side to almost everything, because there's a negative side to almost everything. Nobody's perfect, and you can be on the lookout for evidence to prove it.

While irreverence has you looking for the negative, defective, and embarrassing side of things, the joke must be "on" some person or some group. Rather than rely on a plainly aggressive insult, which few will find comfortably humorous, your humor will be more palatable if it points out that there is at least a little vanity, a little greed, a little dishonesty, a little laziness, and a little stupidity in everyone. Will Rogers said that everybody is ignorant, only on different subjects.

Develop a sense of fun. Most of us are too tense, and we've forgotten how to play. The psychology of humor is not much more complicated than the psychology of "just kidding" or "poking fun." I enjoy using puns, even if it's just for the pun of it.

Humor also needs an element of fair play. It should throw a punch that's hard enough to get a laugh but soft enough to be accepted as appropriate for the occasion and the target. It's a little like the golfer who has to swing hard enough to clear the lake, but easy enough to stop on the green. The gentle dig that mixes harmless fun with veiled flattery will earn you warm laughter and affection.

Much of the clever wit turned out by funny thinkers comes from divergent thinking. One of the world's experts on the subject is Dr. Edward de Bono of Britain. He calls it *sideways* or *lateral thinking*. But it could just as easily be called upside down, backward, or circular thinking. It's the opposite of convergent thinking, in which the thinker proceeds logically in a straight line, from point *A* to point *B*.

The divergent thinker starts out with the notion that maybe *A* and *B* don't have anything to do with each other. Or maybe *A* should come after *B*. He uses free association and other presumably disorganized techniques. Thus he turns up thought clues, unusual connections and angles, and anything else that may lead to logical, but unusual, solutions and ideas.

De Bono explains that serious, logical, straight-line thinkers are tyrannized by usual and old ideas. They frequently come up with the same idea others have already thought of because they keep using the same straight and narrow logical path other thinkers have used and reused. For instance, when people want to solve a difficult problem, they usually say, "Let's get down to brass tacks." I ask you, what's wrong with copper tacks, steel tacks, sailing tacks, income tax, syntax, and contacts? Maybe there's more than one alternative.

Sometimes divergent thinking can turn up consequences that are highly literate commentaries on our way of life. Here's an example. The modern bathtub was invented in 1856. The telephone was invented in 1870. This means that for fourteen years one could soak peacefully in the tub without being called to the phone.

Many funny ideas, especially those based on divergent thinking, are inherently surprising. Many others are not, and so must be made surprising by the manner or context in which they are presented. Putting it another way, an important element of humor is a sense of "setup" or deception: "She uses convenience foods a lot. She has what you would say a *Birdseye* view of cooking." That idea has inherent surprise. Frequently a deceptive buildup consists of an apparent compliment preceding the punch. "Have you all noticed Joe's new tie? Isn't that some tie? It . . . it *is* a tie, isn't it, Joe?"

Even when the basic idea does have built-in surprise, it will get a better response if even more deception is added. Here's one example: "You'll be happy to hear that my brother finally found a job. He didn't *get* it, he just *found* it." The basic idea that finding a job isn't getting a job is an unexpected twist. The train of thought necessary to get from A to B makes it even more funny. Here's another example: "I wish I could thank each and every one of you personally for helping me win this election. I wish I could thank all of you. Obviously that would be ridiculous, because many of you were no help whatsoever." A sense of deception tells you that almost any idea can be made surprising if it is preceded by a misleading idea and delivered in a misleading manner.

Humor depends on clear, quick communication of words and ideas. Jumbled word order or scrambled thoughts force your listener to stop, and even to back up, to figure out what's going on. And so, in using humor you face all the challenges of serious communication, only with greater intensity. But the rewards of learning to use humor are worth the effort.

FIVE ACTION STEPS TO HELP YOU TO DEVELOP AND USE HUMOR

1. *Use incongruity.* Lead people to believe that you're going to say something very logical, then say something different or unexpected. Example: "The mayor of New York should have the fluency of Henry Clay, the solidity of Daniel Webster, the firmness of Andrew Jackson, and the digestion of an ostrich."

2. *Use exaggeration* to strengthen your point by stretching the truth. To illustrate his three-time loss as a candidate for president, William Jennings Bryan used this anecdote: "A woman was so fat that she had to get off the streetcar backward. She had tried three times to leave, but each time she was helped on again by someone who thought she was entering instead of leaving."

3. *Use understatement* to represent something as less than it really is. Referring to the bombing of Pearl Harbor, Winston Churchill said, "They [the Japanese] have certainly embarked upon a very considerable undertaking!"

4. *Use irony* to say something that is the opposite of what you mean. Mark Twain said, "It's very easy to give up smoking. I've done it a thousand times."

5. Look for the situations in your everyday life where you are taking yourself too seriously, and see the absurdity of the situation. This will lead to greater self-awareness, which leads to greater self-confidence, which leads to improved performance.

We can measure our growth as we observe our use of humor in our everyday life. Humor seems to grow out of an emerging wisdom. The *power* of humor recognizes this humanness. With this we can achieve a new level of success as we laugh with and at ourselves. And as we encourage others to laugh with us, all of us benefit as we share our humanity.

Chapter 10
HOW TO DEVELOP THE CHARISMA OF A SUPER PERSUADER

It's easy to spot. Jesse Jackson has it. So does Elizabeth Taylor, Magic Johnson, and Johnny Carson. The Kennedy family hands it down from generation to generation, as if it were part of the inheritance.

It's charisma—that special magnetism that draws us to someone for reasons we can't always explain. It's almost like a magic circle of attraction.

Charisma is hard to define because it entails so many different qualities. It can mean personality, charm, magnetism, and even pizzazz. But it all boils down to the ability to win the confidence of the people in your environment.

Charisma is different things to different people. It depends on your point of view. For instance, Michael Jackson has tremendous appeal with the younger people, but their parents may not be drawn so readily into his magic circle of magnetism.

There is some disagreement over whether charisma is all chemistry or whether it can be acquired. A Yale psychologist calls charisma one of those factors that has a whiff of magic about it. It has a reputation of being somehow mysterious, and being more chemistry than psychology. Therefore, people tend not to study it, and that adds to its mystery.

FIVE LEVELS OF HUMAN NEEDS

More and more people are now coming to believe that a little conscious effort can create a charismatic aura. Psychologist Abraham Maslow contended, in his theory of human needs and motivation, that needs aren't just something people feel when they're deprived of the basic necessities of life, such as food and water. Instead, he claimed that there are higher needs that motivate all of us to actualize our potential as human beings. From this thesis Maslow formulated a needs hierarchy consisting of five levels. The *highest* level is self-actualization. And it is the traits of people at this level of needs that make up the charismatic. But let's start at the beginning. Maslow points out that self-actualization is our highest need, but it's a need that only becomes *prominent* when other lower needs have been adequately met.

Our lowest, most basic needs are *physiological*. These include the need for food, water, sleep, and sex. These needs are prepotent over all the others. That is, we will not be concerned with anything else as long as we are racked by hunger or dying of thirst.

When these needs are adequately met, a second set of needs arises. These are the *safety needs*. This includes our need for security and stability. They show up in our desire for structure and order, and in our need to predict what will happen to us. Our safety needs include our need to be protected and cared for, and also our need to protect and care for others.

The third set of needs are *belonging and love needs*. These can be seen in our desire for community and our desire to have a place we can call home. It shows our need for close and meaningful relationships with friends and family. Widespread loneliness in our society today reflects the difficulty we have in fulfilling our love and belonging needs.

The fourth set of needs are *esteem needs*. These include the need for a healthy sense of self-respect and to be respected by others. They also include our needs for feeling competence, mastery, and achievement.

Finally, the highest need is for *self-actualization*. This is the need to become the person we were meant to be, to utilize our talents and capabilities. It is to know ourselves and others more fully, and to contribute in a positive way to the world around us. It is the need that motivates us to want to see more clearly, to live calmly yet dynamically, and to understand deeply.

THE CHARISMATIC PERSONALITY OF THE SELF-ACTUALIZED SUPER PERSUADER

With self actualization, and charisma, as our final goal, let's take a closer look at what it means to be self actualized. There are many characteristics of charismatic people. The most important are: (1) high levels of self-awareness and self-confidence; (2) good interpersonal relations with others; (3) a belief and a willingness to stand up for values such as honesty, justice, and goodness; (4) higher levels of generalized creativity; and (5) more peak experiences.

The fundamental attribute of the charismatic person is the ability to perceive more accurately oneself, others, and the world in general. Because the basic needs are fulfilled, or quieted, the perceptions of a person at this level are accurate and untainted by lesser considerations. This accuracy, in turn, leads them to greater self-awareness and greater feelings of independence and confidence. Charismatic people, more than most people, know *themselves*—who they are, what they believe in, what they value. In social situations they are more independent. They trust their own judgment. There is an old Zen saying, "Eat when you're hungry, sleep when you're tired." It means that we should listen to ourselves, and trust our internal messages.

Charismatic people *are* more independent, but they maintain good relations with others. They experience extremely deep and strong relationships with those closest to them and have benevolent, brotherly feelings toward people in general. In relating to others, they are able to say both yes and no. They can say yes to relationships because they do not fear closeness. They can say no because they know who they are and what is not good for them. Because they have self-esteem, they are not afraid to be honest with others and let others get to know them. Because they accept themselves, they are better able to accept others. The net result is a heightened capacity to develop and experience loving human relationships.

Charismatic people have very high values and are willing to stand up and be counted for their convictions. Even if a situation arises when standing up for their values is not the popular thing to do, the charismatic person will stand up and speak out for those values.

Another trait of the charismatic individual is creativity. I'm not referring to the specialized creativity that results in great works of art or scientific discoveries, but rather to a generalized creativity—a way of viewing and approaching life. It involves the attitudes of openness and flexibility, along with a willingness to take risks by stepping into the unknown. The point is not what the charismatic person *accomplishes,* for the occupation may be quite menial. Instead, it's that attitude toward life that allows you to see new possibilities in situations. Charismatic people often come up with creative responses to everyday problems and situations.

Finally, charismatic people are more open to, and have more, peak experiences. Maslow describes a peak experience as "the most wonderful experience or experiences of your life; happiest moments, ecstatic moments, moments of rapture, perhaps from being in love, or from listening to music or suddenly 'being hit' by a book or a painting or from some great creative moment."

During peak experiences we feel differently. We feel a personal power, as if all our abilities and potentialities have come together for one magnificent moment. During the peak we are more open to experience and feel more fully functioning, more creative, and more individual. At the same time we feel that the whole universe has come together and that we are one with it. We feel integrated and whole, and life seems more worth living than we ever imagined it could be.

Peak experiences are not only powerful when they are happening. They also leave powerful, positive aftereffects. Generally speaking, peak experiences enable us to view ourselves in a more positive way and give us a more positive view of life. They can release greater creativity and spontaneity and permanently alter how we view things.

WHY DO SO MANY PEOPLE LACK CHARISMA?

If becoming a person with charisma is just a step beyond the fulfilling of lower needs, and being charismatic has so many desirable characteristics, why don't more people achieve it? What holds us back?

The greatest difficulty most of us have is in fulfilling our needs for safety and security. This means we usually live with two strong and conflicting needs—the need for safety and security, and the need to use our talents and abilities and take risks. Just as we have a natural desire to reach out and express our potential, we also have a natural desire for order and comfort in our lives. We like the familiar, even when it is not the best for us. (How else could we explain the many people who stay in jobs that are not satisfying or fulfilling? For what other reason other than the need for safety, security, and predictability of the familiar, do so many people stay in relationships that are not satisfying?)

Growth does not typically happen by quantum leaps. It happens through hundreds and thousands of little decisions and actions we take every day. It's the decision to be honest with a friend, to do something to improve ourselves, to spend more time with those we love. It is the decisions that we believe, in our deepest selves, to be good for us, that produce growth. When we do not listen or act on the messages we get from our inner selves, it is usually because our needs for safety and security outweigh our desire to grow. We are afraid others will not approve of us if we act on the inner voice, or we do not have the confidence that the inner voice is telling us the right thing to do.

LISTENING TO YOURSELF

One of the most important things we can do to become charismatic is to learn to listen to our true inner selves. Our goal is to tune in to ourselves, listen to what we hear, and act upon it despite what others may think.

Don't be concerned that this will make you self-centered and uncaring of others. As a human being, you are entitled to live your life as you believe it should be lived. Other human beings should extend this right to you, and you should extend this right to them. This does not mean you have the right to willfully harm others. In fact, when you listen to your inner self and accept the responsibility for your own life and the way you are living it, you will not want to harm others. You will find that sarcasm and manipulative communication are no longer fitting for you to use. You realize that others are not living your life *for you*—that you are living it for yourself. They are not responsible for your happiness or unhappiness— you are.

MAKING GROWTH CHOICES

Each day we are confronted with countless opportunities to make *growth choices*. If we don't have our focus on growth, these opportunities are lost. To cultivate the growth habit, we must become better at recognizing our opportunities. Take today as a starting point. Review the day in your mind. Can you identify any situations with opportunities for decisions that would have helped your personal growth? Perhaps someone at work criticized you and you responded by criticizing them back. Could you have used a more productive response? Perhaps you're interested in changing some habit that you find undesirable. When confronted with the choice of continuing the old habit or doing something differently, how did you respond? Perhaps you laughed at an off-color joke that was offensive to you. Perhaps a situation came up in which you would have to control your temper. How did you respond? Continue reviewing the day to identify opportunities for growth changes and improved communication. You may want to list them on a sheet of paper so that you can be aware of how many there are in a typical day. In the future, be alert to opportunities for growth choices as they present themselves.

In social situations, listen to your inner voice. You are offered dessert. Do you really want more food, or would you rather say, "No thank you"? Every day many situations arise in which we have the option to respond without thinking or to tune into our true inner wishes and desires. Starting today, promise yourself that you will stop and tune into your inner voice before making snap decisions and responses.

Besides making decisions to voice your opinions, you also have opportunities every day to express your true self. How often have you wanted to get to know someone better but didn't have the courage to walk up and introduce yourself? How many times have you hesitated to speak out and say what you really believe and let others know what you think and feel? We get to know one another by what we tell each other. The only way to have the kinds of close relationships we all crave is to have the courage to let others get to know what we honestly experience, think, and feel.

ENTHUSIASM CREATES CHARISMATIC POWER

People with charisma also have enthusiasm. What is enthusiasm? The word is defined as "a force or quality through which human beings exercise and perform acts with great inner power and desire." A person with enthusiasm exudes vital qualities of warmth, drive, and exuberance.

The first part of enthusiasm is desire. If a person wishes to become president but doesn't really believe it's possible, the wish will never become a driving force. Desire is transformed into drive when a dream creates a passion for action.

At this point there is no more painful struggle to reach a goal. We are ready to pay the price for our success. Much physical, mental, and psychological coordination will occur before the dream is realized, but the first step is desire.

The second part of enthusiasm is confidence. A person who has low confidence does not feel or act enthusiastically. Positive self-confidence is a protective barrier against negative feelings and obstacles. It gives the security that frees the imagination.

Positive self-confidence begins with knowledge. This is achieved through the willingness to learn effectively and comprehensively. We should never avoid a learning opportunity. Knowledge is followed by understanding. Understanding is a sense of awareness that activates constructive, positive thinking. For example, if we want to do something, knowledge of how to do it is important, but it is not enough. We need to understand the process, the results, the objectives, and the functions involved in completing that project.

Positive self-confidence finally appears when mental harmony develops. Disturbance, logical or emotional, often results from ignorance and misunderstanding. Mental harmony, however, is a normal consequence of knowledge and understanding. It is a feeling of satisfaction that allows self-confidence to grow.

CHARISMATIC ENERGY OF THE SUPER PERSUADER

The last part of enthusiasm is energy. After desire is built and positive self-confidence established, our mental world produces energy powerful enough to survive even the strongest doubts.

An enthusiastic person, a person with charisma, displays vast quantities of energy. Other people who observe this individual find themselves saying, "I just don't know how he (or she) does it!" What these observers fail to realize is that the enthusiastic, charismatic person is driven by boundless psychological, mental, and physical energy. Such energy must be expended. The successful person channels it into enthusiastic action.

CHARISMATIC POWER THROUGH INNER SECURITY

The trademark of our modern age seems to be *insecurity*. The poor wonder how they will survive the inflationary erosion of their income. The rich pay security firms more than seven billion dollars a year to safeguard themselves and their property.

The pressures of life affect us all, but we don't all feel them to the same degree. For those who have learned to accept uncertainty and possibly even enjoy it, the challenge of each new day can be faced with a sense of adventure rather than defeat. It's all in how you respond.

Maxwell Malz, author of the popular book *Psycho-Cybernetics*, estimated that 95% of us have at least mild feelings of inferiority, the primary cause of insecurity.

So let's admit that we sometimes feel inferior, and that makes us insecure. Face that fact and you have taken the most important step toward overcoming the problem. Psychology tells us that neurotic anxiety, so prevalent today, results from our efforts to deny the basic uncertainty of life. When we maintain the illusion of security in an insecure world, we fall deeper and deeper into difficulty.

Since nearly all of us have feelings of insecurity, there is no reason to be ashamed of them. Famed Vienna psychiatrist Alfred Adler said, "This feeling of inferiority is the driving force, the starting point, from which every childish striving originates." Some of us *use* it as a motivating power to achieve greatness. Others hide behind their fears and withdraw from the difficulties of life. If we just keep going, despite uncertainty, each success builds further self-confidence. This strengthens our ability to handle the next challenge that comes our way.

Without inner security, no amount of success or wealth can still those nagging voices in our minds. Those nagging voices plague the businessman who comes up with great ideas but is reluctant to express them because they might sound silly. Lacking the self-assurance to say what he thinks, he gets angry at himself for not speaking up, especially when someone else is congratulated for expressing the same thought. At the opposite pole, insecurity can appear in the one who knows it all. This is usually the person with a blustering, overbearing personality that hides a fearful person inside. We've all met both types, but maybe we didn't understand them.

Focus on your strengths, not your weaknesses. It may come as a surprise that people are concerned more about their own insecurities. They may not even be aware of your weaknesses! You are the only one who really cares about them. Change what you can and accept the rest. This will help to develop your charisma and build your super persuasive power.

FIVE ACTION STEPS
TO INCREASE YOUR CHARISMA

1. *Be yourself*. The mystic Ram Dass said, "If you learn tricks, you will be a caterpillar that flies. But you will not be a butterfly." There is real value in accepting yourself, imperfections and all. The heart of the problem is doubt about your self-worth. Many believe that they have value only in terms of what they produce for others. As human beings, we all have infinite value and a unique contribution to make. Stop measuring your worth against others, and start appreciating your special talents.

2. *Be open to others*. So often we try to draw within a protective shell that no one can penetrate. But when you reveal yourself to others, blemishes and all, they will overlook your imperfections and appreciate your good qualities. Face your shortcomings and allow yourself to laugh at minor mistakes.

3. *Expect others to like you*. An apologetic attitude is self-defeating. Don't assume everything you do is wrong. If you naturally expect others to like you, they probably will. And you'll like them too. Surveys show that the best-liked people are those who like others. Nothing will build your charisma faster than having a circle of warm, accepting friends. People walk through the door of your expectations.

4. *Turn outward*. Resist the tendency to become preoccupied with yourself. Many people are so wrapped up in their own insecurities that they fail to notice the needs of others. Charismatic people are able to forget their own problems and get involved with other people. They help others

for the sheer joy of doing it, without calculating the return.

5. *Work toward a goal*. Insecurity feeds on aimless drifting. Dedication to a purpose in life is the fastest way to forget your weaknesses and use your strengths for a worthwhile cause. Success itself is not a goal because at the top of the heap is the most insecure position of all. People with charisma *use* success as a means to accomplish what has meaning for them. The reward is lasting satisfaction.

The word *charisma* has its roots in Greek mythology. Charis is one of the three graces, and refers to the divine gifts and attributes we each have within us. These gifts, when recognized and actualized, enable us to live and communicate with total love, power, and self-confidence. In a nutshell, this describes the personality of a dynamic Super Persuader.

Chapter 11
ADVANCED COMMUNICATION TECHNIQUES OF THE SUPER PERSUADER

The great nineteenth-century preacher, Lyman Beecher, called persuasion "logic on fire." That is the essence of what the persuader tries to communicate. People need to be appealed to on a rational basis, giving them justification for their beliefs, but they must also be given an inspiring goal or example to motivate them in the direction you intend.

A good example of this process is a trial lawyer's summation to the jury. He carefully and logically builds a case on the evidence, and then describes the evidence in human terms, trying to create an emotional attachment between the jury and his client. He often ends with a passion-filled plea for justice, using words that convey innocence, fairness, and other strong emotions. Should the logical evidence, the emotional appeal, or the passion be missing, chances are that the jury will not be persuaded.

A persuader helps people to define the number of viable choices available to them. He or she accomplishes this by helping them to eliminate undesirable choices. Because people need this service, they will listen to you and be persuaded to your point of view if you are skilled at presenting and clarifying their choices.

SIX WAYS TO INCREASE YOUR PERSUASIVE POWER

Here are some ways to be more persuasive in everyday situations.

1. *Use the home-turf advantage*. Suppose that you are going to have a talk with a neighbor whose tree overhangs your backyard. Should you go to his house or invite him to yours? Many people can be more relaxed and persuasive in their own surroundings than in someone else's. That's why a good negotiator always strives to have important meetings held in *his* office. Research shows that this technique really does work.

    Two psychologists at Johns Hopkins University rated sixty students for dominance—the ability to influence others. Then they divided the students into groups of three. Each group had one member low in dominance, one average, and one high. The students were then asked to discuss and agree on which of ten potential university budget cuts would be best. Half of the groups met in rooms of their most dominant member, and half in the rooms of the least dominant. On the average, the guests' views came around to the host's point of view, even if the host was low in dominance and the guests opposed them at the onset. When you can't hold a meeting in your home or office, look for neutral ground so that the other side won't have the home-turf advantage.

2. *Look your best*. In a small town where I used to live, an artist often got so steamed up about local government decisions and issues that he would speak out at the governing board sessions. He would come unshaven, in frayed and

paint-splattered jeans, contemptuous of those who dressed up to impress others. He said that those who did were stupid. And perhaps ideally he was right, but he was probably more in the wrong. We like to think that we are more influenced by what a person *says*, rather than how he *looks*, but experiments show that this isn't true.

Sixty-eight volunteers from the University of Massachusetts were asked to approach four passersby to enlist their support for a group opposed to serving meat at breakfast and lunch in the campus dining halls. The volunteers had previously been judged on appearance and assessed on speech fluency, credibility, persuasiveness, and intelligence. The attractive volunteers were far more successful at influencing people than their less attractive counterparts.

Now, this doesn't mean that you can't be persuasive unless you're a knockout, even if you're a genius. What it does imply is that the effort and time that you spend in grooming and looking your best are well worth it.

3. *Identify with your listener.* Whenever your goal is to persuade others, you must phrase your appeal in terms of their self-interests. People are not "driven" by persuasion; they are "won" by it. They are drawn, through their own desires, to satisfy their own needs. What *you* want to accomplish is certainly of interest to *you,* but probably not to them. They are primarily interested in what *they* want, so make sure *your* interests coincide with *theirs*.

As a start, make them like you *personally*. They should feel that you are a part of them, that you share their interests and beliefs. They should be able to identify with you and respect you, even as they sense your respect for them.

You will be more persuasive if you show yourself to be a person more similar to them than different, making them comfortable with you on the basis of shared beliefs and outlook. Keep in mind, though, that this is a matter of emphasis and is not a call for deception. Nor should it be seen as a lack of true conviction; if this were the case, you would not be able to effectively persuade others to follow your lead. The politician uses this tactic of emphasis quite effectively: before a labor audience, he is Mr. Labor; before a business audience, he couldn't be more conservative.

There is a human tendency to believe what someone who is "one of us" says. For example, a brewmaster may be able to tell you lots of reasons why one brand of beer is better than another, but your friends—whether they are knowledgeable or not—will probably have a bigger influence on which brand you choose.

There's more to it than that, of course. A California psychologist conducted some interesting research. He found that top salespeople "match the tone of voice, volume, rhythm and speech of the customer and mirror their body language, posture and mood. Unconsciously they may even breathe in and out with him. (He even has videotape to prove it!) In essence, the best salespeople act as sophisticated biofeedback mechanisms, sending back the same signals the customer is sending to them." For years therapists have been trained to alter their behavior and level of language sophistication to create a comfort zone for their client. This is not an act of insincerity but rather an adaptability to make the client feel more at ease. Again, it is important to identify with your listener.

4. *Reflect the listener's experience.* Mediocre persuaders jump right into their argument; skilled

persuaders first create trust and show empathy. If the other person indicates that he's worried about something, the persuader who says, "I understand why you feel that way. I would too," is showing respect for the other person's feelings and will gain that listener's attention. One of the most powerful persuasion techniques consists of three short sentences. They are: "I understand how you feel"; "I used to feel that way too"; and "then I realized that . . ." And here you present your new point of view.

A good persuader will reflect, not rebuff, the other person's objections to his argument. The skilled persuader restates the objection, allows that it has merit, and only then goes on to show that his own ideas are more cogent. One top insurance agent will readily agree with a customer that life insurance is a terrible investment. Having disarmed the customer and having his total attention, the agent then demonstrates that insurance has a different purpose than investing —that it's a way of protecting against catastrophe, a way of making up for savings or investments one doesn't have. Several studies have shown that when a presentation looks at both sides before coming to the conclusion, it seems more persuasive than one that offers views of only one side.

5. *Make a strong case.* You will increase your persuasiveness if you give your listeners solid information instead of just opinion. When doing so, keep in mind that people who are uncommitted can be as much influenced by the source of the facts as by the facts themselves. In one study at Yale University, two groups of ten volunteers each heard the same factual argument in favor of selling antihistamines without a prescription. One group was given a fictional source called

The New England Journal of Biology and Medicine and was persuaded much more easily than the other group, which had been told that the source was a popular pictorial magazine.

It's not simply that people trust some sources and mistrust others. Rather, when they hear strong, highly credible authorities cited, they're far less likely to defend their preconceptions against new ideas and information. A word of caution: Don't overdo citing experts. Too much information may make the listener rebel.

6. *Employ stories and examples.* Suppose you're trying to sell your car to a stranger. Which will be more persuasive, the national figures on gas mileage for your model or the mileage you got on a trip last weekend?

Great persuaders have always known that we are more easily influenced by examples and personal experiences than we are by summarized evidence and general principles. A doctor once advised a friend of mine to take a certain drug for a minor medical problem. My friend asked if it was dangerous. The doctor then outlined the evidence, and my friend felt reassured. Then the doctor added, "I take it myself," and my friend was persuaded.

FOCUS ON THE FACTS

Once you have the attention and trust of your listeners, and they are convinced that what you say really matters to them, you will need to build a solid, logical base for your viewpoint. If your listeners are favorable to your view, your communication should be specific and of a motivational nature. In this instance you should verify what they already consider in some vague way to be true, to bring a passive belief up to the level of an active commitment. Review the arguments in favor of the view that you share, thus reinforcing your listener's beliefs and giving them solid reasons to believe something that previously may have been only a vague feeling.

If your listeners are opposed to your view, be less specific than if they were favorable or neutral. Lead them back to basic principles and establish a ground of common agreement —even if it is only the agreement that there is a problem that must be solved. *Your* goal is to open their minds at least enough to consider what you have to say. Thus your thrust should be to reduce the confrontation by focusing on the facts that are indisputable, and basic views that are common to *both* views.

DEALING WITH EMOTIONAL COMMITMENT

People usually have an emotional commitment to their own views and often see an argument against these beliefs as a personal attack. Remember that persuasion is not argumentative. It does not try to batter down the opposition. Rather, as its Latin origin suggests, it is convincing "by sweetness." Try to direct the listener's attention away from their "rightness" and toward a consideration of whether or not the facts are correct.

If your listeners are neutral or apathetic, your first job is to convince them that the subject really affects them. If you are confronting a problem, show how this problem relates to their lives and interests. After you have established the importance of the problem, present the possible solutions, with arguments for or against each one. Explain the impact of each solution and demonstrate why yours is best. You will generally be more effective if you present your side *first*, dispose of any major counterarguments, and then conclude with a summarized statement of your viewpoint.

USING PROPS TO INCREASE YOUR PERSUASIVE ABILITY

Great persuaders often use anecdotes, charts, graphs, or concrete examples to make their view even more attractive. One father was having a discussion with his son about the importance of staying in college. The son was considering dropping out in order to become a ski instructor, and he enthusiastically told of all the fun he would have, though he did admit that he would have to live at a subsistence level for several years until he developed a clientele. The father, realizing that logical points on the long-term advantages of education would not be heard because of his son's level of enthusiasm for the ski-instructor idea, instead wrote two checks to his son. The first was made out for $250,000. As he handed it to his son he explained that this is what he could expect to earn in the next thirty years without a degree in a salable field. The father then handed the son the second check, which was filled out for $500,000. The father said, "This is what you'll have to share with your family for the next thirty years if you finish your degree and work first. Can you really ask your future wife and kids to make that kind of sacrifice so you can have a few extra months of skiing?" The boy sat quietly for a few minutes, then decided to postpone working as a ski instructor until after he graduated some eighteen months later. He later said that he couldn't get the difference in earnings out of his mind. The visual impact was just too great.

HOW VISUAL IMPACT
CAN HELP YOU

It is said that the visual impact of television is so great that it obscures what is being said. Yet the impact of television is but a pale imitation of what the mind can produce when a person's imagination is turned loose.

When conducting psychotherapy with clients who are distressed about their feelings or behavior, I virtually always have them relax with me—often using hypnosis—and then I have them picture the kind of person they want to become. Visualizing what one wants to become is a powerful motivating factor in actually working to reach the goal. You can also use this guided-imagery technique to help your listeners formulate a better mental picture of how payoffs will personally benefit them when they accept your idea. What you succeed in getting a person to bring forth in his mind (through your words) will most likely make the difference between his agreeing with you or refusing to cooperate. Not until he pictures himself enjoying the rewards and anticipating how he will feel when it happens will he be seriously interested.

ASK OTHERS TO TAKE ACTION

It would be foolish for someone to present a persuasive conversation, to go through the tension and uncertainty and not ask the listener to take action. Yet it happens all the time. One research study that followed more than a dozen salesmen for two weeks found an amazing problem. The researchers discovered that on more than 65% of their calls, the salesmen did not ask their potential customers to buy their products. They quoted facts and figures, they displayed samples and charts, and they related warmly to their potential customers.

But they never took out their order pad and actually asked how many of the product the customer would like to have. Thus their effectiveness was compromised.

Many of us do the same thing, and the people we talk to go away from us wondering what the purpose of our discussion was. We do this to avoid being rejected. If we don't ask, we aren't rejected. We would rather not have what another wants than be rejected. What you need to do is to realize that rejections, which will occur less and less frequently when you use the techniques we've just gone over, are really rejections of concepts and ideas, not of you. If you separate people's refusals from you as an individual, those refusals will be easier to accept.

Work the percentages, but stack the odds in your favor by knowing what you are asking for, when to ask for it, and making it easy to picture the benefits you are offering. If you have used this process correctly, you have usually made a friend of your listener. At the very least, this new relationship will leave the door open for a future time when you can ask for cooperation once more.

EXPECT—CLARIFY—CONFIRM

Few people are won over to an important commitment in a single meeting or discussion. They need time to accept your personality pattern and to get past any lack of rapport caused by personality conflict. They need to trust you and to think through the ramifications of your offer. Also, most people fear making a mistake. You can use the technique given here only when you see that your listener is visualizing the rewards and is making commitment statements. To act too soon is to turn him off. To act too late is to miss the tide of his emotions.

When a person nods in agreement, smiles and leans forward as if reaching for something, or acknowledges that the cooperation would please him, make it easy for him to accept your offer and hard for him to reject it. Remember the words *Expect, Clarify, Confirm*. You *expect* that he is intelligent enough to see the benefits of acting in his own best interest. You *clarify* his understanding and resolve any lingering doubts about the importance of acting now. And you *confirm* the value of the mutual payoff and his acceptance of it.

When you are convinced that the resolution you recommend is the one you would want for yourself if the situation was reversed, your conviction will be seen through your nonverbal communication. When you know it's the right thing to do and the listener is agreeing with you, anticipate that his decision is going to be the same as yours and act accordingly. Because you have paid your emotional dues to him while discovering his needs and problems, talked about resolutions and payoffs, checked to see that he understands the advantages of cooperation, and the reward is appealing to him, you have earned the right to advise him. In his mind he has seen what can happen, and he assumes that you'll go ahead and ask for his commitment. He does not feel that he has lost control but that he is making a choice, and it's his choice; he is not being compelled to submit or to make an eternal choice but to choose in a minor way with a supportive friend.

In the past, persuasiveness seemed to be a mysterious and personal gift. Today we know that it is largely the result of certain communication skills and techniques that can be learned. To convince yourself of this, just apply what you have read and see what happens.

FIVE ACTION STEPS FOR USING THE ADVANCED SUPER PERSUASION TECHNIQUES

1. *Gain the home-turf advantage*. Schedule meetings in your home or office, or if that's not pos-

sible, choose a neutral site so that the other side
does not have the home-turf advantage.

2. *Look your best.* Your appearance and grooming
add or subtract from your credibility and the
level of confidence that you exude. Other people
are more likely to accept the ideas of people
who have taken the time to make themselves
attractive.

3. *Identify with your listener* and reflect the listener's experience. The good persuader does not
argue but agrees and guides the thinking of the
listener to another alternative. Try this example:
With your hand, push very strongly against the
hand of a friend. Now release the force and tension; pressing lightly, merely guide your friend's
hand in a circular motion. This is the secret to
effective persuasion.

4. *Present a strong case* using both a rational and
logical justification and a strong emotional appeal or inspiring goal. Support your case with
stories, examples, personal insights and experiences, and visualizations of the expected rewards and results.

5. *Ask for support and action.* When you have presented a strong case and are convinced that the
resolution you recommend is the one you would
want for yourself, if the situation was reversed,
trust that your listener's decision is going to be
the same and act accordingly. Finally, get a firm
commitment for active participation.

The ability to persuade is the basis of the ability to lead.
Learning the techniques of how to persuade others to believe
you, to follow you, and to help you will give you more powerful qualities of leadership and make your ideas irresistible.

Chapter 12
THE SUPER PERSUADER IS A MOTIVATOR

It is very appropriate that we end our discussion of Super Persuasion with the subject of *motivation*. Motivation is the culmination and end result of all the other skills we have studied.

The most sought-after job skill today, and the job skill that can make the most money for you, is the ability to make others want to take action. Supervisors are promoted faster if they can motivate their employees to do better work. Salesmen earn higher commissions if they make their customers want to buy. Teachers get the best positions in their district if they can make the children want to learn.

I don't think this ability is in demand because few people have it but because few people know how to *develop* it. There's no reason why you can't easily learn to use a few basic techniques that will make you an instinctive people motivator.

As you know, nobody willingly lets others order him around. People want to think for themselves. A good motivator get things done by making others want to cooperate. To be a good motivator it's important to understand some basic principles of motivation.

BASIC PRINCIPLES OF MOTIVATION

First of all, people do what they do because they feel comfortable acting that way. When someone's happy with the way things are, he has no reason to change. But if this same person becomes unhappy with his circumstances, he will begin to feel uncomfortable. People *don't like* to feel uncomfortable, and when they feel this way, they're open to suggestion. When they learn a new way to behave that removes the discomfort, they will gladly change their actions; they'll be motivated to act in the new way.

So the first step in motivating others is to make the other person feel uncomfortable about his current actions or circumstances. Second, we need to show him a new and better way to act that will remove the discomfort. And third, we need to stand aside and let him change of his own free will.

As you use these steps, you'll begin developing persuasive power that makes your communication pay off. At first it may seem a little involved, but as you work the steps, they'll seem very natural, and before you know it, they'll become a habit.

STARTING THE SPARK

Do you remember how Boy Scouts are taught to make a fire without using matches? First they cut a pile of dry wood shavings, then they strike a flint until sparks fall onto the shavings. Finally they blow on the spark until the shavings start to blaze.

Getting through to other people is a similar process. First you prepare a bed of attention. Then you strike a spark and conversationally fan it until it creates a blaze of interest. To continue the comparison, a spark will burst into a fire faster when the wood shavings are dry and have not absorbed a lot of dampness. Similarly, a blaze of interest is created when the person's mind is "dry" and not absorbed with its own thoughts or emotions. Here are some ways for you to break down the two most common mind absorbers that prevent you from getting the other person's attention.

BREAKING THROUGH THE PREOCCUPATION BARRIER

The first one is to break through the listener's preoccupations. If someone is wrestling with his own problems, he won't pay attention to you unless what you have to say is more important than his thoughts. One way to penetrate a preoccupied mind is to help the other person solve his problem. Say, for example, you walk into Bill's office and he is studying a map. You ask if he's planning a trip, and he responds that he's leaving tomorrow to drive to a distant city. You can respond with your knowledge and suggestions for the fastest route. At this point Bill's mind is free and ready to turn its attention to what *you* have to say. Had you jumped right into what you wanted to tell him, his mind still would have been on the trip.

RELIEVING TENSIONS

Second, it is important to relieve the other person's tensions. When someone's nerves are tied in knots, his mind will be tied up too. So to get his full attention, you must first relieve his tensions.

One of the ways to do this is to set an example by keeping relaxed yourself. Use a quiet, soft voice, slow and deliberate movements, and calm attentiveness toward his personal needs and feelings. Actions like these create a relaxed atmosphere. Also, keep the conversation centered on topics that are safe. Don't discuss a topic that will aggravate or excite him, but talk about relaxing subjects like his hobby or his plans for the coming weekend. There is one exception to this: If he is emotionally uptight about something in particular, then it's often best to let him talk it out. Once he has had a chance to vent his emotions, he will be more receptive to giving you his attention.

MAKING OTHERS FEEL APPRECIATED

Finally, make him feel appreciated. I have never met a person who did not want to be important in some way. And I have never met a person who I could not swing to my way of thinking when I give him that feeling of importance he wanted so much. Even that rare individual who thinks that he does not want to be important still insists on being heard. So everyone wants the attention of other people, whether he wants to admit that or not. He wants to be listened to; he wants to be heard.

You can benefit from that basic desire to be important. You'll never go wrong by doing your utmost to fulfill that basic need. Just knowing a person wants importance is not enough, however. You must show him *how* he can get it. And you must know how to get what he wants before you can ever hope to gain power with him so that you can get what you want too. Here are some ways you can do this.

UNDIVIDED ATTENTION
GETS THE BEST RESULTS

Give the other person your undivided attention. Psychologists, psychiatrists, ministers, business managers, criminologists, marriage counselors, all have come to one simple conclusion in this art of dealing with people: If you really want to get results from an individual, you must master the art of giving them your undivided attention.

It's the only way you can be sure of gaining power with people so you can get what *you* want too. Why is this so? Well, it's really simple. Our actions to attract another person's attention are simply an outward manifestation of our inner desire to be important. We yearn for attention. We want our ideas and opinions to be heard. The desire for attention is present in all of us. If you think not, let me ask you if you have ever been snubbed by a waiter, left standing on the corner by a bus driver, or completely ignored by a salesclerk. Remember what you felt at the time? You know exactly what I am driving at now, don't you?

A good place to start practicing these skills is right in your own home. Start by going out of your way to pay attention to your spouse or loved one. You don't have to buy them gifts every day. Instead, let them know by your *actions* that you know he or she is there; this method will cost you absolutely nothing and is, in fact, even more effective. Say "please" or "thank you" to build mutual respect. When you pass each other in the house, gently brush each other's hand or smile and acknowledge the other's presence. If they're involved in a project, take them a glass of water or a soft drink and ask, "How's it going?" Don't worry about them not being thirsty. They'll drink it just to show their appreciation for you because of your concern and caring. These might sound like insignificant things to do, but they are proof positive to your spouse or loved ones that you love and appreciate them.

This works with children too. It doesn't take a lot of extra effort to give some special attention to your kids. Ask them to play a game with you or go for a bike ride. Pay attention to them and they'll love you for it. A good, healthy game of Ping-Pong with your teenage son will do more to reduce the generation gap than any lecture you can give him in the back bedroom.

FOCUS ON "THEM" INSTEAD OF "YOU"

There is no faster way on earth of driving people away from you than by constantly talking about yourself and your own accomplishments. Not even your best friend can put up with never-ending stories of how important you are. Even he will reach the limit of endurance. The only way you can win lasting friends and gain power with people is to become truly interested in them and their problems. To do this you need to take your mind off yourself and think that other people are just as important as you are.

All of us are self-centered most of the time. To me, the world revolves around me. But as far as you are concerned, it revolves around you. Most of us are always busy trying to impress someone else. We are constantly seeking the spotlight. We continually want to be at center stage. Most of our waking moments are spent in trying to gain attention. But if you really want to communicate with people, you must train yourself to take your mind off yourself. And you can do that by centering your attention on helping others. If you want to understand people better and win their hearts and their support, then you must be willing to help them solve *their* problems, and fulfill *their* needs. Simply tell yourself that other people and their problems are as important as your need to get attention. When you adopt this attitude, meaning that you *believe* it, you won't have to put on a phony face and butter up the other person to make the attitude work. With this new approach you can stop pretending and looking for gimmicks to make him feel important.

I know of no quicker way to insult people than to brush them off or turn away when they are trying to tell you something. Show your consideration by listening attentively and sincerely when someone speaks. Let that person know that what he is saying is important. Pinpoint his strong points by listening and understanding which of his personal traits he is most proud of, and show him that you recognize these traits.

Thus you get through to other people by first clearing their minds of preoccupations and emotional tensions and by making them feel appreciated as people.

PLANTING THE KEY IDEA

Not that you have captured another's attention and interest, you're ready to take the first step toward motivating him—*planting the key idea* that there is a better way of acting than the way he is acting now.

Remember how you learned math and spelling? You repeated the principles over and over. Educators discovered long ago that spaced repetition is a vital link in the learning process. Repetition shouldn't be used in a nagging way; rather, subtle hints should be dropped from time to time, calling attention to the behavior that you want changed—without emotion or judgment. Simply state the fact, as in, "I notice that you don't have that project finished."

HOW TO USE THE QUESTIONING TECHNIQUE

Once you've planted the key idea, guide his thinking with another familiar teaching technique—*the questioning technique*. "Do you agree it's important to have this done on time?" or "Do you think it is important to do it this way?" or "Why do you think it is important that you complete this on time or this way?" This technique is much more to your advantage than lecturing, because when you lecture, people will feel that the idea is being forced on them, that they have no say in the matter. It becomes a "have to." And when someone feels he has to do something that he has no control over, he will resort to avoidance behavior. Worse than that, if he feels he is being *forced*, he may try to sabotage you. But when you ask questions, people feel that *they* came up with the idea. Congratulate the other person for realizing the importance of the better way of going about some task. You'll be making him aware of new behavior without getting him angry with you for "forcing" him to change.

Next you want him to accept that the new behavior or change is more beneficial to him than the way he is acting. This is where the fireworks can begin, because people don't like to change, so they naturally resist new ways of doing things. But as soon as they can see that the change is more beneficial than their present behavior, they will become dissatisfied with their behavior and they'll feel an inner conflict. This works to your advantage. Since people don't like inner conflict, they will do whatever they have to do to eliminate the anxiety or inner conflict. The idea you planted offers the opportunity for the *resolution* of this conflict. Realizing this, the person will want to accept the idea. So keep talking persuasively about the idea. Keep motivating him to act in the new way. You want him to become so completely involved in the new idea that he finally accepts it as his own and acts on it.

Be suspicious if someone immediately agrees to change. Most people just don't accept new ways of changing that fast. Many people do play the game of false acceptance, however, their reasoning being, "Why let myself in for a lot of grief? I'll agree to whatever he wants and act as if I've changed for a while, then when he's forgotten, I'll go back to my old ways." A good solution is for you to address the problem by saying, "It's going to be easy to slip back into your old patterns because habits take a conscious effort to break. What are you going to do to remind yourself to do it the new way?"

Since you know that people resist new ideas, why not draw this resistance out into the open where you can handle it conversationally in a positive way? To do this, keep asking questions and encourage the voicing of any feelings about the new idea. Keep yourself under control. Don't argue against his objection or try to prove him wrong. This positive approach helps you because it keeps him open-minded. If you start by attacking his objections, he may correctly think to himself, "Why bother talking, he's not interested in how I feel. He just wants me to agree with him." If he feels this way, he will hold back his true feelings.

LOGICAL AND EMOTIONAL REACTIONS TO OBJECTIONS

As he voices his objections, the key questions to ask yourself are, "Is he overreacting to the change I suggested?" and "Is he being too emotional in his resistance?" If you answer no to these questions, chances are his objections are logical ones. If you answer yes, then he is reacting emotionally. Here are some ways of spotting emotional reactions: his voice is higher pitched or louder than usual; he jumps quickly from one objection to another as if he were trying to overpower your idea by the sheer number of things he can find wrong; he's stubborn in holding to his previous thinking and refuses to consider your idea; or he brings up objections that are unrelated while hiding his *real* objections.

The easiest way to counter a logical objection is to face facts with common sense. Patience and a listening ear are your two major weapons when you face emotional objections. The first thing you should do is to encourage the other person to sound off as much as he wants to. Just listen quietly and empathetically until the full force of the emotion is gone. You can't get through to someone who is emotionally uptight.

After he quiets down is the time to make him realize that he is taking an unreasonable position. Do this by discussing his comments calmly, not by attacking his objections or accusing him of being emotional. Your chances of success are greater if you can get him to admit to himself (not necessarily to you) that he is being unreasonable.

Respond quietly and calmly. Tell him that you are not forcing him to change and consider him to be a very important part of the family unit, business, office, project, etc., and that his responsibilities are important. As you calmly and logically discuss his objections he will begin to feel uncomfortable and he'll begin to see that his objections are not supported by fact. He'll begin to see he was overreacting and will start to change his attitude. During your motivating conversation keep projecting sincere interest in the points he raises and keep showing respect for him as a person. Never put him down or make fun of his remarks, but rather listen to him with the same honest concern that you would like if the situation was reversed.

SUPER PERSUADERS MOTIVATE OTHERS TO ACTION

Once your listener has been conversationally motivated by your idea, getting him to change often requires no more effort than simply asking him to take action. Salesmen call it "asking for the order." And this is where many people fail when trying to motivate others. They present a positive and beneficial case for change, they show the other person what he will gain if he makes the change, and then they stop there. If you want to motivate someone, you must ask him to take action. Firmly ask the other person what you want him to do. Only when he responds to your request will you have completed your job of conversationally motivating him to take action. Ask him when you can expect this new behavior or routine to start, and have him accept personal responsibility without your having to monitor or remind him. If he refuses to act, you haven't satisfied all of his objections. Return to the previous steps and get him to discuss the idea once more. Ask questions that encourage him to bring up any objections he didn't voice earlier. Then handle these objections in the same way you handled his original ones. Once this is done, ask him again to carry out the new behavior, action, or routine. Make sure you get his commitment to action.

Once you have motivated someone to act in a new way, everything will go along fine—for a while. But then the original enthusiasm may begin to wane. This is called the *thinning-out period*. You may find him slipping back into his old ways. This is the time to follow through, to keep him motivated. Do this by reminding him that he was right in making the change in the first place and review the benefits he will gain by completing or continuing the change. You might say "I certainly like the way you can accept responsibility." This rewards him and gives him recognition for making the change. Continued recognition will keep him from slipping back into his old habits.

Following are some other points to help you motivate others, especially if you are in business.

Manage by objectives. Give people a clear idea of the results you want to achieve and then leave the methods up to them. Suggest methods, rather than dictating them, with the understanding that people are free to devise something better. Consult people affected by a problem or a proposed change and ask their ideas, regardless of whether you think you need them or not.

Enrich jobs by delegating as far down the line as possible. If a worker is capable of being trained to make a certain decision intelligently, why have it referred to a supervisor? If a supervisor is capable, why have it referred above him?

Guide your people so that they think of constructive solutions you may already have in mind, rather than simply presenting them yourself. If they feel it is their idea, they will be motivated to take action.

Do as much as you can to eliminate needless rules and

allow people as much freedom and mobility as possible, as long as they produce good results and don't interfere with others.

Remember, the more freedom you can give a person to do a job the way they'd like to, the more satisfaction they will get from it, and the better they will do it.

FIVE ACTION STEPS TO HELP YOU MOTIVATE OTHERS TO ACTION

1. Make the person you wish to motivate uncomfortable or dissatisfied with his current actions or circumstances.

2. Show him a new and better way that will remove his discomfort.

3. Listen to his objections and help him come to his own conclusions, through your guidance, that his objections are unfounded.

4. Ask him to take action. Give him complete credit for changing, but make sure he knows that you are aware of his accomplishments. Recognition is a powerful motivating force.

5. Follow through during the thinning-out period by reminding him that he was right in making the change in the first place, and review the benefits he will gain by completing or continuing the change.

In doing this, you will master the most sought-after job skill today—the ability to make others want to take action. And that's the primary goal of the Super Persuader.

Using these techniques will insure your ability to motivate, persuade, and make others *want* to take action. This is the Magic Power of Super Persuasion!